Wulfric reached out a hand, pulling her to a stop. His eyes were unusually serious. "Edwynn is not the man for you."

Surprised, Arietta could only stare. She loosened his hold from her arm and pushed him away with unnecessary force. "That is not for you to say."

His look darkened considerably at her physical rejection. Before she could ascertain his intentions, he grabbed her by the forearms, pulling her close. She did not resist him, except to glare into his icy blue eyes.

"You need a man to keep you warm on long winter nights," he murmured roughly.

She lifted a brow, tilting her head arrogantly. "I have a man who will do so."

Wulfric drew in a jagged breath. He pulled her closer, studying her face, and Arietta thought it time to put a stop to this odd conversation. She tried to free herself from his hold, but once again his superior strength had its way.

Wulfric dropped his lips to hers, and suddenly the whole world receded into nothingness. Arietta struggled against him briefly, but she couldn't deny the intense feelings engendered by his kiss. Her struggles lessened, then ceased altogether, until she was returning his kiss with a fervor she hadn't realized she possessed.

When Wulfric finally pulled back from her, his eyes had darkened with his feelings. "You need a man," he told her huskily, "who will make your blood sing when he kisses you."

Arietta took several deep, steadying breaths. When she pushed against him, he released her instantly. "I am not an animal, Wulfric. God gave me the ability to use my own mind, and He would expect me to keep my promises," she told him, appalled by her unexpected response to his kiss.

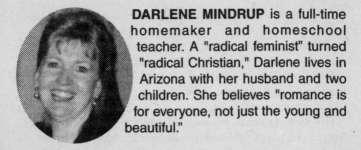

DARLENE MINDRUP is a full-time homemaker and homeschool teacher. A "radical feminist" turned "radical Christian," Darlene lives in Arizona with her husband and two children. She believes "romance is for everyone, not just the young and beautiful."

HEARTSONG PRESENTS

Books by Darlene Mindrup
HP207—The Eagle and the Lamb
HP224—Edge of Destiny
HP243—The Rising Son
HP280—A Light Within
HP315—My Enemy, My Love
HP336—Drink from the Sky
HP376—Mark of Cain
HP419—Captive Heart

Don't miss out on any of our super romances. Write to us at the following address for information on our newest releases and club membership.

Heartsong Presents Readers' Service
PO Box 721
Uhrichsville, OH 44683

Viking
Pride

Darlene Mindrup

Heartsong Presents

A note from the author:
I love to hear from my readers! You may correspond with me by writing:

Darlene Mindrup
Author Relations
PO Box 719
Uhrichsville, OH 44683

ISBN 1-58660-337-X

VIKING PRIDE

All Scripture quotations, unless otherwise noted, are taken from the King James Version of the Bible.

All of the characters and events in this book are fictitious. Any resemblance to actual persons, living or dead, or to actual events is purely coincidental.

Cover design by Lorraine Bush.

PRINTED IN THE U.S.A.

prologue

872 A.D.

A quiet little village lay nestled among the green hills on the west coast of Wessex in what would some day be called England. Smoke rose in grey spirals through the small holes in thatched roofs. Everywhere, people milled about, unhurriedly attending to their daily chores.

The peace was suddenly shattered by one piercing blow from a horn some distance away. One sharp blow, then silence.

The people stopped to stare fearfully in the direction of the sound, waiting for further blasts. None came.

A soft murmur grew into overly loud whispers.

"The Norsemen!" one man declared loudly, causing almost instant panic.

Another man scoffed, lifting his pitchfork and shaking it at the wind. "Do not be foolish! The warning for the Norsemen is three loud blasts."

"Why would the sentry make only one blow?" another woman asked with trepidation. "One blow is a symbol for nothing."

As the people debated, a young woman hurried inside her cottage, slamming the door behind her. Her long dress swished around her feet, hindering her progress.

"Arietta," she called, her voice strident with fear. "Arietta, where are you?"

A girl's face peeked out from the loft above. An impish grin tugged at a rather large mouth. Freckles danced across the child's face, her dark hair spilling across her shoulder in one long braid.

"Here I am, Gwyn."

"Come down quickly."

Puzzled, Arietta tilted her head to the side. "Why?"

Gwyn sighed with impatience. Dropping her basket on the table, she climbed the ladder that led to the loft and glared fiercely into her sister's emerald green eyes.

"Listen to me." Gwyn shook Arietta's shoulders for emphasis. "I want you to go to our cave and hide there. Don't come back until I come for you. Do you hear?"

The fear in her sister's voice mixed with the furious command widened the younger girl's eyes. "Why?" Arietta's voice was almost a whine as she grudgingly followed Gwyn down the ladder. Something was wrong. Never had her sister spoken to her in such a tone of voice.

Taking Arietta by the arm, Gwyn jerked her toward the back door. "For once, would you stop asking why and just do as you are told!"

She opened the back door, searching fearfully with her eyes one way, then another. She took her sister by the shoulders again, staring fixedly into her eyes. "Remember what I said. Do not come back. No matter what you hear. No matter what you see. Do not come back!"

Arietta tried to pierce through her older sister's matching green gaze, but she couldn't fathom the reason behind this unusual directive. Conditioned to obey, she nodded her head slightly in acquiescence.

For a moment, Gwyn's composure crumpled. She pulled the girl close against her, sudden tears filling her eyes. "Remember, I love you. I will always love you." Turning the girl around, she added, "Now, run! And do not look back."

Arietta started off at a slow trot, then stopped and turned.

"Go!" Gwyn commanded more harshly. "Run!"

Arietta did as she was bade. Her feet flying through the familiar brush, she was some distance away before she heard the first screams from her village. She stopped, frozen with terror, trying to decide if she should disobey and return to her sister.

Gwyn's words echoed through her mind with urgency. *Run! And do not come back, no matter what.*

Gwyn was not to be disobeyed. Arietta hurried on and made her way carefully to the cave on the hill. It had been a haven for Arietta and Gwyn for years. Though Gwyn was ten years older than her own eleven, they were close, as only two lonely children without a mother could be.

The screams were silenced here. Nothing could be heard save the trilling of the birds in the shedding red, orange, and yellow leaves of the trees around her. When a sudden breeze rifled the branches, the colorful leaves floated to the ground.

Shivering from fright, she stopped at the entrance to the cave and looked back. Smoke rose in billowing black waves from the village behind her. Turning toward the ocean, she looked down the hill. Directly below her, in the lapping water of the channel, lurked a Viking longboat. Several men paced along its deck, unaware of Arietta's scrutiny, their shields close at hand, hanging from the sides of the ship. Her green eyes grew dark with suppressed fury, a bubbling hatred forming in her chest. Were she a man, she would strike them all dead.

Suddenly, more men burst through the trees, carrying their booty with them. Many had women thrown over their shoulders, their terrified screams going unheeded by any save the lone child standing on the hill above their heads.

Arietta recognized her sister among those being thrown into the longboat. With a terrified wail that sounded more like an animal in pain, she flung herself toward the edge of the cliff.

Silence surrounded her as all eyes turned her way. The Vikings began gesturing toward her, and some started to move in her direction. A sharp command brought them to a halt. Arietta couldn't hear what was said, but it had an instant affect on the warriors. They hurriedly climbed aboard their ship and made ready to leave.

Gwyn's eyes met Arietta's, and the child read in them her

terror and resignation. With each stroke of the oars, the ship moved farther away until Arietta could no longer make out her sister's features.

Moaning, Arietta dropped to her knees. Burying her eyes in her fists, she rocked back and forth, tears running in rivulets down her cheeks, then dropping to the cold earth beneath her.

one

Ten years later

Three long blasts from the sentinel's horn sent Arietta ducking out her front door to stare off into the distance. Already the other townspeople were dropping what they were doing and heading for the green forest surrounding their little village. Long ago they had learned that discretion was the better part of valor where the Norsemen were concerned, and it was better to flee and see another day than to stay and fight, and meet your eternity.

Though it had been ten years since Arietta had last heard that sound, the remembered terror of that time now filled her heart with panic, and to no small amount, rage.

She hesitated but a moment before turning and fleeing through the woods to her favorite hiding spot. As she ran, images of that day so long ago filled her mind. Never would she forget the sight that had met her eyes on her return to the village.

The village church had been ruthlessly vandalized and plundered, and Father Edward lay dead on the stone steps. He had been foolish enough to believe he could reason with the Danish savages, and in the end, he had paid with his life. Still, it spoke well of the priest's valor.

Half of the village had been ablaze, the burning fingers of flame lifting high into the afternoon sky. For those who had not fled in time, the circumstances had been dismal. Many had died, many others had been taken prisoner during that Viking raid.

The village had been caught unaware, due in no small part to Vengus the watchman's penchant for ale bringing swift destruction on his head. They had found him slain, his horn laying close to his side. Since that time, the others who served as watch had taken the job very seriously. After such a long period of time though, and what with King Alfred having defeated the Viking Gunthrum, they had once again grown complacent in their vigil.

Arietta pushed her way through the surrounding brush and into the cave. She was tempted to go to the edge of the cliff and look down at the waters below, but too well she remembered the last time. Only by God's grace had she been kept from the hands of the heathens.

She flung herself down on the earthen floor, leaning back against the cold stone wall. She shivered with remembered images and the pain that always followed.

Time eked away, but she was oblivious. Probably she was free to return to the village, but she really didn't want to. She was afraid of what she might find. It had taken much time to rebuild after the last raid from these wrecking Vikings, but they had managed to survive and even prosper, which was probably why they were being raided again.

Dark anger burned in her heart until she felt as though she would surely be consumed. Brother Bertrand from the abbey had been teaching the people of the village the Scriptures as a concession to King Alfred's desire to educate his people, but some of the Scriptures were hard to hear. Especially the ones about forgiveness.

Even now, after ten long years, love for her sister Gwyn washed over Arietta in painful waves. Her father had been devastated by the loss of his oldest child, but not more so than Arietta. Gwyn had been the only mother she had ever known.

Then just a year ago, Father had died in a hunting accident, and she had been left completely alone. Before Father had died he had arranged a marriage between herself and Edwynn, the village smith. Now she wished he had waited, for even though she was alone, she had no desire to marry.

She tensed when she heard rustling in the brush outside the

cave. Fingers digging into the hard earth, eyes wide with sudden fright, she listened intently for other sounds. It was but a moment until she heard voices, and her heart thundered with terror.

Her throat closed with choking fear as a figure emerged from the sunlight into the dark interior. It was a woman, her hair woven into two long braids hanging over her shoulders. Arietta couldn't see the color, nor the features, but she instantly recognized the style. This time, the Vikings had brought their women with them.

Arietta pulled a knife from her boot, waiting in silence. Though she could see the woman clearly, the woman could not see her until her eyes adjusted to the darkened interior. Curling her fingers tightly around the hilt of the knife, Arietta tried to decide if she should attack or not.

"Arietta?"

Arietta felt herself grow cold all over. Her mind refused to function clearly. The voice sounded like that of her sister, Gwyn, but that was not possible.

"Arietta, are you in here?"

With a strangled cry, Arietta jumped to her feet. She stood, her chest heaving with tightly controlled feelings.

"Gwyn?"

The sound came out a strangled whisper. The woman moved closer, and a shaft of sunlight from behind lit her face.

"Gwyn!"

Dropping the knife, Arietta flung herself at her sister. She had no idea how this miracle had occurred, but she lifted her thoughts in silent praise to the great God of heaven.

Gwyn held her close for a moment, then pulled away. She took Arietta by the arm and moved her to where the sunlight was filtering into the cave.

"Arietta? Is it really you?"

Arietta gave a choked laugh. She had dreamed of this moment so often, she wondered now if this was reality or her own fanciful imaginings.

"I could ask you the same!"

Gwyn lifted one hand to her mouth, her trembling fingers spread over her parted lips. She stared at Arietta in disbelief.

"Oh, my! I cannot believe it is you." Tears sprung to her eyes, but she swiftly brushed them away. "I left a girl behind, and now I come home to find a full grown woman."

Arietta clasped both of Gwyn's hands in her own. "How? How is this possible?" She looked beyond to the entrance to the cave. "We heard the horn."

Gwyn stared hard at her sister, and Arietta suddenly became uncomfortable under that look.

"There is much I need to tell you," Gwyn told her. "But I am not certain where to begin."

Arietta barely heard the words. "I cannot believe you are home. I just cannot believe it!"

Gwyn smiled briefly. Her look went beyond Arietta to the cave entrance. "Wait here. There is someone I want you to meet."

Puzzled, Arietta watched her sister disappear through the entrance. She blinked her eyes at the now empty portal, wondering if the last few minutes had been a figment of her overactive imagination. Suddenly, Gwyn reappeared. A very large man entered the cave behind her, and Arietta's blood froze in her veins.

The man stood where his golden hair and beard were highlighted by the waning afternoon sunlight. His piercing blue eyes fixed on Arietta, and she had to swallow twice before she could utter a sound.

"A Viking!" Suddenly intense green eyes fastened on Gwyn. "You have betrayed me!" Arietta trembled all over with mingled rage and fright.

Gwyn shook her head slowly, her hands outstretched in silent supplication. "No, Arietta. This is my husband. . .Sidroc. We have come back to stay."

&

Arietta retrieved her knife and followed her sister down the hill, Sidroc bringing up the rear. She could feel the Norseman's eyes on her back, and the hair stood up on the back of her neck.

When they entered the village, Arietta stopped, staring at the chaos surrounding her. Vikings and villagers alike were mingling together. Arietta recognized some of the women who had been taken from the village years before. They stood among their kin, hugging and crying with joy.

Sidroc passed Arietta to stand next to his wife. He glanced down at her, and Arietta couldn't miss the look of adoration that her sister gave the giant. His own returning smile was full of tenderness. He glanced back at Arietta, and Gwyn turned to her.

"We heard about King Alfred's defeat of Gunthrum and that a treaty had been signed and the Danelaw established." Since King Alfred's defeat of the Danes several years ago and the establishment of a boundary that fairly split England into two parts, the Vikings and English had been living in relative peace, each on their own side.

Arietta watched her sister, suddenly suspicious. Had these Vikings come to help their brothers overthrow the rest of England? She looked beyond her sister and counted. If these men were here to make trouble, their numbers were decidedly low. She could see only fifteen Norsemen. Still, others could be hiding, ready to strike at any given time. Her look went back to Gwyn, and her racing thoughts stilled. No, though Gwyn obviously adored her Viking husband, Arietta couldn't believe her capable of such perfidy.

One of the Norsemen detached himself from the others and crossed to stand before them. His gaze fastened on Arietta and held. His look traveled over her, and she knew in that one brief scrutiny that the man had missed nothing, from her raven black hair, to her small, leather-clad feet.

He stood as tall as Sidroc, the wool tunic tightening over his muscular arms when he crossed his arms over his chest. His golden hair hung below his shoulders, meeting his equally golden beard. As was so common of the Vikings, his eyes were a glacial blue.

Gwyn smiled at him, then turned her smile on Arietta. "This is Wulfric, Sidroc's brother." She pulled Arietta forward. "Wulfric, this is my sister, Arietta."

Frosty green eyes met glacial blue. A slow curve started at the corner of the Viking's mouth, then traveled along until it turned into a full sardonic smile. "Greetings." His English was clear and faultless.

Arietta gave him no returning smile. Her look was full of loathing, and one blond brow lifted on the Norseman's face.

"Arietta, where is Father?"

Arietta pulled her gaze from Wulfric's and turned to her sister. There was no emotion on her face, and her voice was hollow when she answered. "He is dead. He died last year."

Arietta barely registered her sister's quickly indrawn breath. She saw Sidroc lay a comforting hand on her shoulder. He looked into her eyes and spoke something to her in the Norse language. Gwyn nodded, the tears that she had decried earlier now running in a silent stream down her cheeks.

Sidroc pulled her into his arms and whispered words that Arietta couldn't understand, but Gwyn obviously could. She calmed under his ministering touch. Arietta was amazed. The stories she had heard of the Norsemen and the atrocities she had witnessed firsthand had led her to believe that they had no heart. Sidroc's tenderness toward her sister was both unexpected. . .and unsettling.

She turned away from the tender scene and encountered Wulfric's enigmatic stare. Arietta nearly ground her teeth in annoyance when he smiled knowingly. Though she couldn't speak Norse, she could easily read his looks. He knew the hate she was harboring in her heart.

Gwyn pulled away from her husband and laid a hand on Arietta's arm. Arietta wasn't certain what message was in her sister's eyes, but she could feel herself responding to it, nonetheless.

"Arietta, we want to build our home here with you and the others. May we stay with you until Sidroc and Wulfric can build us a house of our own?"

Before Arietta could answer, they were interrupted by angry voices from the crowd of people in the village square. "No! You cannot stay here! Take your heathen husbands and be gone. Go to the Danelaw where you belong."

A woman tried to intervene. "But Thomas—"

"No, Wife. I tell you, she is no daughter of mine. Let her go and live among the heathens she has embraced."

Another man stepped forward. "Be still, Thomas. You do not speak for us all. I welcome my Anna back and her husband as well."

The atmosphere grew heated with angrily exchanged words. Some were in favor of accepting the returnees, but others were too filled with fear, or hatred, or a mixture of both. Arietta could well understand their dilemma.

Brother Bertrand finally stepped into their midst. "Now, now. Let us first see if these. . .these infidels are willing to give their allegiance to our Lord Jesus Christ."

Arietta watched in stunned surprise as Gwyn shoved herself forward and faced them all, her hands placed firmly on her hips. She glared at each villager in turn, her green eyes flashing fire, the epitome of a Viking valkyrie.

"My husband is a Christian, as are many of his people."

"What kind of Christian steals women and murders priests?" Thomas sneered, stepping threateningly close. In the next instant he found himself facing a large, muscular chest. Thomas stepped back quickly, the sudden fright evident in his eyes.

Sidroc faced them all, his angry gaze touching each one until they unknowingly took steps back out of his reach.

"Take your vengeance out on me if you want to," he thundered in perfect English, "but lay a hand on my wife, and you will find yourself standing before your maker sooner than expected."

Gwyn touched his arm gently. "Please, Sidroc."

He glanced down at her and read the message in her eyes. Nodding, he stepped slightly away, but all there knew he would not hesitate to do as he suggested.

"Give us a chance," Gwyn begged. "We have missed our homes and families, and our husbands have been kind to us, kind enough to allow us to come home." She turned to Thomas and spoke quietly. "We want to share your grandchildren with you."

The color drained from the Englishman's face, and his look went to his daughter. Gwyn motioned to the forest behind them. "Bring them."

A woman emerged, followed by several children of various ages. Their frightened looks scanned the stupefied people before them, but their mothers beckoned them forward reassuringly. Two children hurried to Gwyn's side, and Arietta had to sit down on a stump, her legs suddenly unable to support her.

Gwyn smiled at the children, then at Arietta. "Bjorn, Helga, this is your Aunt Arietta."

They stood shyly beside their mother until, at a harsh prompting by their father, they moved to Arietta's side.

Arietta glared at Sidroc to let him know that she didn't appreciate his assistance, then smiled hesitantly at the children. The girl could be no more than six, her golden hair mixed with strands of red. She had her father's blue eyes. The boy, probably eight years of age, held himself proudly. Though his hair was flaxen like his father's, his eyes were the green of his mother's. He crossed his arms over his leather-clad chest and gave Arietta a stony look.

Without meaning to, Arietta found her look lifting to Wulfric. The boy reminded her much of his uncle. Wulfric smiled slightly, and she realized that he had read her thoughts accurately. She pulled her gaze back to Helga, smiling at the child's bright look.

Brother Bertrand cleared his throat, and everyone turned to listen.

"God has given us a great opportunity to share His Word with others. Let us not give in to hate and prejudice, which are the works of the devil. We should welcome our prodigal daughters as God welcomes us."

Aelfric, the shire's ealdorman added his voice to that of the monk. "I agree. King Alfred has made a treaty with Gunthrum, and they have agreed to live in peace. We can do no less."

Though there were grumbles, most were in agreement. Slowly, the square emptied as villagers took their families to their homes for the night. The waning sun stood just above the horizon, and little daylight remained.

Arietta turned to her sister. "Come with me."

Gwyn and her family followed Arietta through the village until they reached her home. She preceded the others through the door, quickly lighting a tallow candle that rested on the oaken table.

The two Norsemen dwarfed the dwelling, making it seem much smaller than it had before. Both Wulfric and Sidroc were studying the room with a thoroughness that caused Arietta a slight twinge of alarm.

Gwyn stood looking around her with delight. "It looks much the same as when I left."

"When you were taken, you mean," Arietta practically snarled. She fixed her look on Sidroc, and the man's eyebrows raised slightly at her venomous gaze.

"Sidroc had nothing to do with that," Gwyn replied. "I will tell you all about everything later, but right now, my children arc tired."

Instantly contrite, Arietta smiled at the two younger ones. "Of course. They can have Father's bed. You and I can share ours, like we used to."

"Perhaps she would like to sleep with her husband."

The quiet words held animosity. Arietta turned to Wulfric and saw that his face was as dark as a thundercloud. The man's gleaming eyes spoke of anger held tightly in check.

Sidroc motioned him to silence. He turned to his wife.

"We can discuss these things on the morrow. Right now, let us get some rest."

When his angry blue eyes met Arietta's, she felt slightly ashamed.

"Where would you have us sleep?" he asked calmly.

Arietta glanced hesitantly from one to the other. Even Gwyn seemed miffed with her.

"The only other place is here, in the main room."

Nodding, Sidroc turned to Wulfric. "For tonight, my brother, we will sleep here. On the morrow, we will build our own house."

Arietta met Wulfric's dark look with one of her own. She lifted her chin a notch and turned away. "I will fix us something to eat first," she told Gwyn quietly.

Gwyn looked relieved. "Thank you. What can I do to help?"

Together they moved to the kitchen area and began to slice and butter bread. Before long, it was as though time had turned back, and they were once again two carefree girls fixing a meal for their father. They giggled, and Arietta felt the tension and anger drain from her. This was Gwyn, her dearly loved sister, the one she remembered.

She was jolted out of her musings by a rough Norse voice, and reality suddenly intruded. Gwyn looked up from where she was preparing vegetables and answered her husband in the same tongue. Arietta felt suddenly left out.

Gwyn placed the food in wooden bowls and handed one to each man. She then prepared food for her children, and finally for herself and Arietta.

Arietta took the bowl, resentful that the Norsemen should be fed before the children, but she realized that this was their way. Many in England held to such a belief themselves, that the man should come first. Having lived on her own for so long, she had all but forgotten.

The meal was uncomfortable for Arietta. Wulfric stared at her the entire time until she almost choked on her food. When she caught his eyes, she noticed a look in his that she couldn't interpret, but it left her shaking. He seemed particularly fascinated by her hair, so black that it shone with blue highlights. Her father had told her that she had Spanish blood in her from long ago. Though others in the village had various shades of hair color, she was the only one set apart by such a striking tint.

Arietta had always thought that she would give everything she owned if she could be as fair of feature as the other village maidens, but never would she have changed her hair. It hung long to her waist in a curly black mass, and it was her one vanity. Now she heartily wished it was any other color than what it was, for Wulfric's intense scrutiny suddenly made her want to pull it out by its very roots.

After the meal, Gwyn helped her children prepare for the night. Arietta could hear her mellow voice as she told them a nighttime tale. The words were foreign to her, and she realized that Gwyn was once again speaking Norse. It aggravated her beyond measure. If they wanted to live in England, then let them speak as English.

She turned to retrieve a bowl from the table and found Wulfric standing behind her. Startled, she dropped the knife she was holding.

They both bent to reach for it at the same time, only Arietta's hand closed over the handle first. She held the knife in her hand, contemplating the man in front of her. Ever so slowly, her eyes went to his bare throat. Evil thoughts jumped into her mind, and she had to shake her head to rid it of such unseemly ideas.

She lifted her eyes to Wulfric's and found him once again watching her, a knowing smile curling his lips. His gleaming eyes told her that he accurately read her mind. Biting her lip, Arietta quickly rose to her feet.

When Wulfric rose to stand beside her, he towered over her small form. There was a challenging glint in his eyes that couldn't be missed.

"Wulfric."

He continued to watch Arietta for some seconds before he finally turned to Gwyn. She handed him a blanket, then handed one to Sidroc as well.

Gwyn placed her palms on her husband's chest and smiled into his eyes. "Goodnight, my husband."

Sidroc's eyes flicked quickly to Arietta before he pushed Gwyn gently away. "Goodnight, my wife."

Looking hurt and puzzled, Gwyn called to her sister. "Come, Arietta."

Arietta quickly followed in her sister's wake. Turning at the ladder to the loft, she found Wulfric's burning eyes still watching her.

two

The first rays of morning light had yet to make their appearance when Arietta opened her eyes the next day. She lay on her straw mattress staring up at the thatched roof of her cottage and thought about the things her sister had shared with her the night before. During that conversation, some of her anger and hatred toward Sidroc had slowly disappeared.

Her sister lay breathing quietly beside her, and Arietta turned toward her. In the dim light from the still full moon, she could see that Gwyn had changed little over the last ten years. Her long auburn lashes fanned across her cheeks, her soft mouth slightly parted. Her hair fanned out in wild disarray across the pillow.

Arietta sighed. She was truly beautiful. No wonder the Norseman had been smitten.

Gwyn had told her that when she had first arrived at the Viking village after her abduction, she had been allotted to an older woman as a slave. Terrified because of the stories she had always heard and unable to understand the language, she had stood before a large crowd of ogling men and fought to keep from bursting into tears. Drawn by the struggle he could see in her emerald green eyes, Sidroc had taken one look at her and fallen instantly in love. He had redeemed her from the other woman at a great price.

When Gwyn spoke of her husband, a wealth of love warmed her voice. His love and concern for her had won Gwyn's heart, and they had been married. It was Gwyn who had introduced Sidroc to the Lord Jesus, though missionaries had been to Norway long before. Although there were some Christians, most still held to the pagan Norse religion. Little by little, they had converted others until the group who had landed on this shore were, for the most part, Christians.

Gwyn had shared with Arietta that some of the others would be leaving to travel farther to a settlement in Iceland. One of those would be Wulfric. Arietta found that, for some reason, she didn't quite like the idea.

Impatient with her thoughts, she pushed back the blanket and carefully climbed from the bed. Having lived in the house all of her life, she made her way unerringly through the dark to the ladder that led to the floor below.

She allowed her eyes to adjust to the room, then carefully searched for Sidroc and Wulfric. She found them sleeping peacefully, one in front of each door, their axes clutched firmly in their hands.

Swallowing hard, Arietta moved cautiously toward the kitchen area. She had to step over Wulfric to reach the bowl with the *gist*. Taking the bowl with the leavened dough, she turned and yelped with fright when she was confronted by a tall, hulking form.

Had Wulfric not reached out to grab the bowl, she would have dropped it for certain. She stepped away from him and backed against something solid. Turning her head, she found herself staring into a broad chest. Yelping again, she launched herself away from both men.

"What goes on here?" Sidroc demanded.

Early morning sunlight was just beginning to filter into the room. Sidroc's eyes met those of his brother. Wulfric shrugged.

"The maid awakened me."

Arietta glared from one to the other. "I did not mean to, but I *do* have chores to attend to."

Relaxing, Sidroc let the point of his ax drop. Arietta noticed that Wulfric also was clutching a weapon. The thought of what might have happened chilled her. She raised uncertain eyes to her brother-in-law and was surprised when he smiled reassuringly.

"I am sorry. We did not mean to frighten you, but we are both light sleepers."

Arietta eyed Wulfric with open hostility. She would have to remember that in the future.

"Sidroc?"

Sidroc turned to find his wife standing at the foot of the ladder, her sleepy eyes going from one to the other in question. Sidroc held his hand out to her, and she quickly came to his side. "I am afraid that we have frightened Arietta."

Gwyn glanced at the ax clutched in his hand and smiled sardonically. "I wonder why?"

Arietta studied Sidroc curiously. "Were you expecting trouble?"

Wulfric answered for him. "These are troublesome times. It is best to be on your guard."

"Yes. We know." When Arietta's eyes clashed with his, her message was unmistakable.

Without answering, Wulfric handed her the bowl he had saved. Slowly she took it from him, glancing quickly away when she noticed his sharp-eyed scrutiny once more studying her. She colored hotly, realizing that she had left off her tunic and stood before them all clad only in her *cyrtel*. She had been alone for so long, she had grown accustomed to performing her morning tasks without adding the extra tunic overgarment.

"Excuse me," she told them all and hastily went to retrieve her overdress. When she returned, she found the others huddled over the kitchen table. Gwyn looked up at her and smiled. "Sidroc and Wulfric would like to find an area where they can build us a house. Who do we need to see?"

"You are welcome to stay here for a time," Arietta answered grudgingly.

After a moment of silence, Sidroc answered, his tone speaking of his irritation. "I think not."

Arietta tried not to look at Wulfric. She had had a taste of his anger the night before, and she knew he would be just as angry now at her lack of hospitality. She was disturbed by it herself.

She sighed, looking at her sister. Gwyn's eyes held a silent rebuke. "What I mean is, you may stay here until I can make other arrangements. Then the house can be yours."

Wulfric's eyes narrowed. "What other arrangements?" he asked, just as Gwyn exclaimed, "I cannot take your home!"

Arietta looked from one to the other. "It is your home too," she answered quietly. "Besides, I promised Edwynn, the smith, that I would marry him. We have been waiting until my twenty-first birthday, but now that you are here, I will tell him that we can marry sooner."

The long silence that followed was broken by Sidroc. "That is not necessary. We would not wish to rush you into anything."

Arietta cast her gaze to the ground. "It is all right. Edwynn will be pleased. He has been after me for some time to move our marriage ahead."

Sidroc and Gwyn exchanged glances. Gwyn nodded her head slightly toward the door, and taking his cue, Sidroc turned to his brother. "Let us gather our supplies from the boat and see how the others have fared."

When Arietta looked at Wulfric, she was surprised at his darkening countenance. He turned abruptly and followed his brother out the door.

Gwyn pushed her long, auburn hair over her shoulders and motioned to the bowl Arietta held clutched in her hands. "Let me help you with that."

Together they worked to make the day's bread. While Arietta added the flour to the gist, Gwyn gathered the *quern* and the wheat kernels to begin grinding grain for more bread. It would take more than one loaf to feed the hungry hoard that had descended on this house.

Gwyn placed the kernels between the two stones, the smaller on top. She watched her sister while turning the handle. "Tell me about this Edwynn. I do not think that I remember him."

Heat flamed in Arietta's cheeks. She dropped the ball of

dough she had formed into the trencher, and placing it on the floor, she began to knead it without looking at Gwyn. "You would not know him. He came to Knarrstow a few years ago. He is a *ceorl*, so he is free to go where he chooses. He chose to come here because Knarrstow is so close to the iron bogs."

Gwyn dropped more kernels through the hole in the top of the stone. "I see," she said and began grinding again. "Since he is a smith, of course that would be useful."

Something in her sister's voice caused Arietta to pause in her work. She tilted her head slightly, studying Gwyn, but could see nothing in her face to suggest that her words were anything other than what they were meant to be.

Gwyn looked up and caught her eye. "And what of this betrothal?"

Not wishing her intuitive sister to guess at her feelings, Arietta began to knead the dough with ferocious concentration. "Father and Edwynn were friends. It was Father who suggested the marriage, and Edwynn agreed."

Gwyn laid her hand over Arietta's to stop her furious movements. Taking a deep breath, Arietta looked up. "But do you *love* him?"

Arietta got quickly to her feet. Taking the dough, she formed it into flat rounds ready for baking. "What does that have to do with anything? Did you love Sidroc when you married him?"

Rising to her feet, Gwyn placed her hands firmly on her hips. "That has nothing to do with this. My situation was much different."

Arietta sighed. "I beg excuse, Gwyn. You are right when you say so."

Gwyn took both of Arietta's hands into her own. Green eyes clashed with green eyes. "I sense reluctance on your part, Arietta."

They were suddenly interrupted by the two children thundering into the room. Gwyn hugged them both close, though Bjorn pulled quickly away, frowning. Gwyn tussled his hair.

"Are you then too old for a mother's love, my son?"

"*I* am not," Helga disagreed.

Gwyn smiled and hugged her again. "Are you hungry?"

Both nodded solemnly. Arietta sliced them a hunk of bread and added some cheese. Taking their meal, the two children quickly sat at the table and began to munch silently.

Gwyn exchanged glances with Arietta. "We will talk later."

Recognizing her sister's words as a threatening promise, Arietta turned away and went out the back door to the oven enclosure. She knelt to light the fire in the clay oven and sat staring at the flickering flames.

What Gwyn had said was true: she *was* reluctant to marry Edwynn. Not that there was anything wrong with him. He was a fine man, strong, handsome, and even wealthy. He was well respected by everyone in the community, but she sensed something not quite right about his spirituality.

Years ago, she and other young people in the community had been trained by Brother Bertrand to make copies of the Scriptures. Although she could not read the letters and words she so diligently copied, she'd listened to Brother Bertrand explain what they meant and had grown to know and love the Lord. She wanted to be His *gebur,* His slave. But Edwynn was impatient with such thoughts. He wanted her to be *his* slave, and his alone.

Taking a few kernels of wheat, Arietta threw them into the oven to test the temperature. After several seconds, they burst open, letting her know that the oven was quite ready. She raked out the fire and the ashes, then placed the stone with the bread on it into the oven opening.

Sitting back on her heels, she bit her lip in agitation. Life had suddenly become much more complicated, and she wasn't quite certain what to do about it.

When she returned to the kitchen area, she found the children gone and Gwyn busily kneading another loaf of bread. She glanced up at Arietta's entrance.

"Where are the children?" Arietta asked.

Gwyn continued her kneading. "They went to find their father."

"Alone?"

Gwyn smiled slightly. "They will be all right. They know where to find the ship."

Before Gwyn could continue her earlier interrogation, Arietta took control of the conversation. "Tell me about the north, Gwyn. What is it like?"

Patting the dough into a flat loaf, Gwyn took her time answering. She stopped, her eyes suddenly distant and sad. "Life there is not much different than here. Everyone tries to do their best to survive another day."

Arietta jerked her gaze back to her sister. There was pain in Gwyn's voice. When Gwyn finally looked at Arietta, she seemed somehow remote. "I had another child. He died when he was only three years old."

Shocked, Arietta placed a comforting hand on Gwyn's arm. "Oh, Gwyn. I am sorry."

She shrugged philosophically, dusting the flour off of her hands. "That is life, Arietta. Even here, it is much the same."

Arietta couldn't argue with that. Gwyn's look became intense as she added, "But you can survive if you have someone who loves you."

"I do," Arietta answered quietly.

Gwyn's shoulders relaxed, though something odd flashed through her eyes. "I see. I did not know. You sounded as though this Edwynn had no feelings for you."

"I was not speaking of Edwynn."

Gwyn pulled out a chair at the table and sat down. She motioned for Arietta to do the same.

"This sounds very curious, Arietta. You have a man pledged to marry you, but another man loves you? Why can you not marry him?"

Arietta smiled gently, her green eyes glowing with hidden delight. "The man I speak of is the Lord Jesus Christ. With His love, all things are possible."

Gwyn returned her smile slowly. "I agree. But it does not hurt to have a man's arms to hold you close when trouble comes."

"Like Sidroc?" Arietta questioned slyly.

A full smile stretched across Gwyn's face. "Exactly."

A commotion outside brought them both to their feet. Arietta hurried to the door, her sister close behind her. When she threw open the portal, she was surprised to find a number of people hurrying past and heading for the village square. "Something has happened," Arietta said sharply.

Both women joined the rushing throng. A large group had gathered around the shire's ealdorman. He was motioning the crowd to silence.

Arietta felt a presence and turned to find Wulfric behind her. He glanced at her briefly before focusing his eyes on the shire's lawgiver. Sidroc had joined his wife, a child clinging to either hand.

"I have spoken with Eorl Dorvald," the ealdorman began. "He has agreed to allow the foreigners to live among us on his land on a few conditions."

Murmurs started among the crowd. Arietta glanced at Wulfric and noticed that his face seemed cast in stone.

"They are to be given the status of *kotsela* and will be given their duties later."

Sidroc lifted a brow at his wife. She looked hesitant to answer his unasked question, so Arietta explained. "It means that you may live on the land and pay no rent. But you will have duties to perform for the Eorl."

"And will we be free men?"

Arietta exchanged glances with Gwyn. She nodded her head slightly in answer to his question. "Yes, but you must serve the Eorl if he calls."

Sidroc's blue eyes grew cold. They reminded Arietta of the ice that formed on the water in the winter. He handed his children to their mother, his very posture growing tense.

Angry shouts erupted from the crowd. Before long, the

whole assembly was in danger of starting a small war.

Wulfric stepped forward, hefting his ax. "We are no man's chattel. We will be free or die in the attempt."

The ealdorman paled considerably. Many stepped out of the hulking Norseman's way.

Arietta moved to his side, looking directly into his eyes. He hesitated but then gave way.

"What the Eorl has proposed is no different from what you would demand if this were your own country."

There were several murmurs of agreement, and Arietta continued. "The Eorl has not asked that you be *gebur,* unlike what your people had in mind for my sister."

Arietta heard her sister's sharp intake of breath at the reference to slavery. She glanced at her briefly but returned her angry look to the Viking. Wulfric's eyes blazed with unconcealed fury. Arietta was not unaffected by his anger, but she promised herself that he would never know it. She tucked her trembling hands into the folds of her tunic to keep them from his all-seeing eyes.

The ealdorman made a placating gesture. "Only the king has the authority to grant land ownership."

After a moment, Sidroc nodded his head at his brother. "What they say makes sense. We will try it their way."

As undisputed leader of the group, Sidroc's voice held authority, but many of the Vikings turned their gaze upon Wulfric. He glanced at each one in turn, then jerked his head in a nod. Dropping his ax to his side, he said, "So be it."

Gwyn breathed a sigh of relief, her fingers relaxing their hold on her squirming children. Arietta joined her and listened as the ealdorman made his other demands for concession.

"You must swear fealty to King Alfred and be baptized into the Christian church."

Only Wulfric and two others refused to do so. Wulfric's eyes met Arietta's, and she read again that challenge in them. Of what he was challenging her, she had no idea, but her chin lifted a notch nonetheless.

A rather taciturn group made their way back to Arietta's house. Wulfric and Sidroc dumped their supplies on the floor of the cottage.

"What will you then do, Wulfric, if you will not be baptized and swear fealty to King Alfred?" Sidroc asked.

For some reason, Wulfric's eyes fixed on Arietta. She felt her heart give a mighty lurch, and she quickly turned away.

"I am only here temporarily," he replied. "Godfred, Ingvar, and I will be leaving before long to go to the Danelaw, and from there, to see if we can arrange passage to Iceland."

"Are you certain you wish to do that? You could live here with us."

Arietta met his eyes again. The intensity of his gaze sent tingles all the way to her toes. "I think not," he replied, still watching her. He smiled at his brother. "But I will stay until you get settled and no longer need me."

"Then you will be here forever," Sidroc told him playfully.

They exchanged smiles, and Wulfric knelt in front of his nephew. "How would you like to come with me?"

"And me?" Helga pushed her way forward, her cloth doll clutched in her arms.

Bjorn shoved her aside. "You are a girl! You cannot come with us."

Tears pooled in the young girl's eyes, and her bottom lip began to quiver. Arietta moved to comfort her, but Wulfric gathered her into his arms before she had a chance, giving his nephew a telling glance.

Bjorn hung his head, looking thoroughly chastened. "I beg excuse," the boy said sullenly.

Arietta hastened to intervene. "Perhaps Helga would like to come with me to look for mushrooms."

The child's eyes lighted, and she looked to her mother for permission. Gwyn nodded. "I will come along also."

Sidroc crossed his arms in relief. "Then I will go with Wulfric, and together we can choose a sight for our home."

He kissed his wife as she passed, then pulled her back to

give her a deeper, more lingering kiss. Arietta turned away in embarrassment and found Wulfric grinning at her in amusement. Eyes flashing, she pushed past him.

ᨒ

Wulfric stood with arms folded and nodded his head in acceptance. "It is as good a sight as any we have seen."

Sidroc nodded. "*Ja*, and it is close to the river."

"That might not be such a good thing," Wulfric told him, suddenly frowning.

Understanding his thoughts, Sidroc answered softly. "The Lord will protect us."

Wulfric lifted a dubious brow. At times he found himself longing for the same kind of assurance his brother seemed to have found in this Christian religion. Unlike many who had been forced to accept it, Sidroc seemed to actually believe, though at times it was obvious he wavered in uncertainty.

"How will He protect you," Wulfric asked, "when He could not save Himself?"

Sidroc smiled wryly at his brother. "And you think Odin has done any better?"

"At least Odin is strong. He would not allow himself to be nailed to a Roman cross."

Sidroc searched his brother's eyes earnestly. "Is it strong to fear death?"

Unable to answer acceptably, Wulfric changed the subject. "What will you do with Arietta?"

"Do with her?"

The teasing light in Sidroc's eyes warned Wulfric. "You know what I mean."

They began their long trip back to the main village. Wulfric lifted his nephew to his shoulders and continued to stride along.

"I like my Aunt Arietta," Bjorn told them.

The teasing light was still in Sidroc's eyes. "I like her too. How about you, Wulfric?"

Wulfric returned his brother's laughing look with a glare.

"I do not find prickly hedges very interesting."

Looking straight ahead, Sidroc shrugged his shoulders indifferently. "For not being interested, you seem to enjoy watching. . .um. . .prickly hedges."

Wulfric paused before he answered. "It is her hair, I think. I have never seen hair that color. It reminds me of Odin's messenger, the raven."

"It *is* unusual."

Bjorn bent his body until he could see into his uncle's face. "If you marry her, Uncle Wulfric, then you could live here. And you could have babies, and I could play with the boys."

Wulfric looked nonplused. Flipping the boy over his head, he returned him to the ground. Not certain what to say to such a statement, he glared at his brother, who was obviously amused by the conversation.

"I will leave marriage to you, Bjorn," Wulfric finally said. "Someday, you can give your father dozens of grandchildren to make up for the nephews he will miss."

Sidroc laughed heartily, thumping his brother on the back. "We shall see."

An ear-piercing scream sliced through the air. Before they could react, Gwyn burst through the trees, Helga clutched in her arms. Her wild eyes met theirs.

"Do something! He will kill Arietta!"

three

When Arietta and Gwyn had separated from the men, Arietta took them on a path that led toward the forest behind the village. They meandered along, content to get to know one another after such a long separation. Arietta swung a basket in her hands, basking in the warmth of the September sun.

Helga imitated her movements with the basket, and Arietta smiled. The little girl was easy to love, and after such a long time of being alone, Arietta found joy in teasing and playing with her niece.

When they entered the gloom of the forest, the air cooled considerably. The smell of loam rose from the forest floor around them, and Arietta inhaled its fragrance. For the first time in a very long while, she felt completely content.

They searched among the ground litter for edible mushrooms, and Arietta took the time to teach her niece which ones were edible and those to stay away from. The girl's intelligent blue eyes gleamed with satisfaction when she chose the right one.

Gwyn smiled when her daughter rushed ahead to the next area. "She has taken to you, Arietta."

Arietta smiled also. "She is a beautiful child, Gwyn. You should be proud."

"I am." Gwyn tilted her head slightly, giving her sister an interrogative look. "And what about you? How many children do you hope to have?"

Arietta flushed brightly. That was something she had given little thought to, for in truth, she had hoped to postpone her marriage indefinitely. "It will be as God wills," she answered finally.

Questions were forming in Gwyn's eyes, and trying to

avoid them, Arietta hurried ahead to join her niece.

"Look, Aunt Arietta. More mushrooms."

Arietta knelt beside the girl, placing an arm around the child's waist. She smiled into the brilliant blue eyes. "You are an excellent mushroom hunter, Helga."

Helga smiled her delight. Both she and Arietta added the plants to Helga's small basket, while Gwyn wandered farther on to look for more.

"Arietta, look! Berries." Pleased with her find, Gwyn began gathering the sloe berries into her own basket. "We can make a pie."

Her attention captured by the offer of juicy fruit, Helga hurried to her mother's spot and began picking berries and shoving them into her mouth. Arietta and Gwyn laughed, and Gwyn tugged on Helga's long braids. "You have more juice on your face than in your stomach."

A sudden rustling in the underbrush caught their attention, and Arietta and Gwyn froze. Helga continued eating berries, oblivious to the women's concern.

A loud snort was followed by the appearance of a bore as it poked its bristly head through the bushes, its white tusks showing in sharp relief against the dark background of the trees. It stood glaring at them, its beady eyes shifting from one to the other.

Gwyn sucked in a breath, her frightened look flashing to her daughter, who stood only a hair's breadth away from the angry creature.

"Gwyn," Arietta told her quietly. "When I get his attention, grab Helga and run."

"What are you going to do?"

Gwyn watched with terrified eyes as Arietta slowly reached to the ground and lifted a small tree branch. The boar focused his attention on Arietta's movements, but his attention quickly returned to the child, who stood whimpering softly only feet away from him.

"Helga, do not move," Arietta commanded.

"Mutter." The child's pleading eyes fixed on her parent.

Gwyn added her own quiet but harsh voice to Arietta's. "Stay, Helga."

Helga obeyed, her terrified gaze shifting to the wild boar, which began scratching the earth with a frenzied motion.

Arietta started to move away from the others, hoping to give them a free path. The boar jerked his attention toward the moving target and squealed angrily, snapping his head up and down.

From her peripheral vision, Arietta could see Gwyn moving slowly toward her daughter. The boar looked their way, and Arietta slapped the stick on the ground to regain his attention. It worked.

The boar's intent became obvious. It was frantic with unbridled anger, and he no longer even noticed Gwyn and Helga.

"Now, Gwyn," Arietta called softly. "Run!"

Gwyn hesitated but a fraction of a moment. Then lifting Helga into her arms, she turned and ran. The boar never noticed.

Arietta glanced quickly around the forest to find some means of safety. Her eyes fastened on a low branch of a tree several yards away.

The boar began pawing the ground in earnest, and Arietta knew she would only get one chance. If the boar's tusks even grazed her, it could cause a ghastly wound that would fester with infection. She had seen too many people with such gashes, and most didn't survive.

When the boar suddenly charged, Arietta threw her stick at it and ran. The stick connected with the beast's snout, and it stopped suddenly, squealing with rage.

Seeing its enemy fleeing, the angry animal charged again. Arietta reached for the tree branch and swung herself up as the boar charged under her, catching her tunic skirt. She heard the rip and felt the pull. Still she hung onto her branch with a grip made strong by fear.

The boar turned to charge again, but Arietta managed to

pull herself up onto the limb of the tree. She grasped the trunk and clung tightly, while the boar circled beneath her, screaming with undisguised fury.

"Go away!" she commanded, but the beast paid her no heed. She hadn't really expected it to. She wondered how long she might have to stay perched in this tree before someone came to rescue her. She lifted a heartfelt prayer that Gwyn would not get lost. After all, it had been ten years since she had last traveled through the dense forest.

Above the sound of the boar's frenzied screams, Arietta heard the movement of brush. Eyes wide with fright, she prayed frantically that Gwyn had not lost her way and turned in a circle.

Wulfric came crashing through the brush, skidding to a stop at sight of the wild boar. He looked up at Arietta, huddled on the tree limb, then quickly turned his attention back to the boar.

Arietta let out a sigh of relief that quickly turned to a choked breath when the animal turned his furious look on the Norseman.

Wulfric lifted his ax, his eyes taking on a savage gleam. His body grew tense in preparation for battle, his breathing coming faster than before. Vacuous, beastly eyes met hardened blue ones.

The boar began pawing the ground in preparation to attack, and Wulfric moved closer, his burning blue eyes never leaving the animal.

The boar charged, but Wulfric stood his ground. When the animal was but an arm's length away, Wulfric swung his ax down, burying it mightily into the boar's skull. The beast fell with a crashing thud, its lifeblood already seeping from its fatal wound.

Wulfric stood staring at it, his breathing coming in short quick bursts. His gaze lifted to Arietta, and he moved across to stand beneath the tree. He grinned up at her, his eyes still glowing with the fever of battle. "You can come down now."

Arietta met his glance and hesitated. He looked more savage

than the wild animal that had chased her up there. He visibly tried to calm himself, and when he reached up to help her from the tree, she hesitated, then slowly swung her legs over the branch and dropped into his outstretched arms. His large hands spanned her small waist.

When Arietta's feet touched the ground, Wulfric's hands remained where they were. The heat from his fingers sent unusual feelings coursing through her body, and she tried to move away. The fingers tightened, causing her to remain where she was. They studied each other for a long moment.

"Are you well?"

Arietta pushed her fists against his unyielding chest. "I am well. Now let me go."

The challenging glint was back in his eyes. His lips curled into a slow smile, and Arietta felt her heart begin to hammer heavily in her chest.

"Wulfric!"

Sidroc's call preceded his sudden appearance. He stopped, almost tripping over the dead boar lying close to his feet. When his eyes lifted to Wulfric, Arietta was standing several feet away.

Sidroc grinned. "It looks as though we will feast tonight."

Gwyn entered the thicket, Helga clutched in her arms and Bjorn trying to see around her. Her pale face grew even paler at the sight of the dead animal. She glanced at her sister. "Arietta, are you hurt?"

Arietta shook her head. "No, I am well."

She watched silently, while Wulfric took some leather straps from the pouch on his belt and tied the boar's feet together. He lifted the animal effortlessly and slung it over his shoulders, then swung his look to her. "Lead the way."

Arietta moved her shaking limbs forward and led them back through the forest until they were in sight of the village. With a squeal of excitement, Bjorn raced ahead, Helga close on his heels, her frightening experience already forgotten.

Trying not to look at Wulfric, Arietta knew that she would

not forget so easily. Something had passed between her and Wulfric in the forest, but since she had had very little contact with men, she didn't quite understand what.

Ingvar and Godfred were waiting for them when they returned to their cottage. Godfred's eyebrows lifted in surprise, a smile curling his bearded lips. "So, you have been hunting without us, eh, Wulfric?"

"It was not my intent," he answered them. "But a happy circumstance, nonetheless."

"Will you join us in celebration tonight?" Gwyn asked them.

Ingvar looked to Wulfric. "Celebration?"

"A homecoming celebration," Sidroc told them.

Ingvar's face took on a closed appearance. "That is what we came to talk to you about," he told Wulfric. "We wanted to know when we would be leaving for the Danelaw."

Wulfric looked first to his brother, then his glance rested briefly on Arietta. "Let us first help the others build their homes, then we will make our way north."

Ingvar seemed less than pleased with the answer, though Godfred was satisfied. He smiled at Wulfric. "Feed me with boar and mead, and I will gladly stay for a time."

Arietta led the way into her small cottage and hastened to the kitchen area while the others sat around the fire pit in the middle of the main room. Their laughter grated on her raw nerves. With shaking hands, she took a bowl from the shelf on the wall and set it on the table. Surprisingly, Helga had remembered to retrieve their mushrooms, and now Arietta began preparing them for the evening meal.

Wulfric came and joined her, and Arietta had a hard time concentrating on the task before her.

"Where should I dress the boar?" he wanted to know.

Arietta couldn't meet his look. She motioned with her knife out the back door. She was unprepared for his gentle touch when he lifted her chin with his fingers. There was a frown marring his brow. "Is something wrong?"

"No," she told him, managing a small smile while at the

same time pulling away from his hold. But something was seriously wrong. Whenever this man came near, the very skin on her body seemed to tingle. Whenever he touched her, her legs turned to jelly beneath her. Somewhere along the line, her feelings of hatred had grown hazy and confused.

He watched her for several seconds, then turning quickly, he went out the door. Arietta marked his leaving with a strong sense of relief. The other men joined him outside, the children following close in their wake, and before long the smell of roasting boar reached into the kitchen from the open doorway.

Arietta took a pan and set it over the fire in the cottage. She added some mutton tallow and waited for it to melt.

Gwyn came and sat across from her, wrapping her arms around her upturned knees. "I should never have left you."

Arietta looked at her in surprise. "Of course you should have. I *told* you to go."

"You might have been killed," she answered harshly. "It was wrong of me to leave you."

Arietta added some crushed garlic to the sizzling fat. She wasn't quite certain what to say. It was obvious that Gwyn was feeling guilty, but if she hadn't fled, Helga might well have been killed.

"Gwyn," she answered softly. "You did right. It was better to risk the one, than endanger us all." She grinned cheekily. "Besides, you know that I can take care of myself."

Gwyn smiled tightly. "That is what made me finally decide. You were always getting into, and out of, trouble." Her inquisitive eyes turned to Arietta. "You have not changed much at all."

The smile slid from Arietta's face. She turned back to the frying pan, throwing in a handful of sliced mushrooms. "More than you can know."

They were quiet for some time, the sizzling of the mushrooms the only sound between them. Finally Gwyn lifted serious eyes to her sister's face. "There is something between you and Wulfric, I think," she stated categorically.

Arietta tensed at the declaration, her insides suddenly full of butterflies. Taking a wooden spoon, she stirred the mixture in the pan. When it was cooked to her satisfaction, she pulled the pan from the flames.

"Have you nothing to say?"

Arietta met Gwyn's look, her eyes holding a warning. "I think you are seeing things that you *want* to see."

Gwyn grinned unrepentantly. "I will have to admit, I wish it were so. You are so right for each other."

Arietta rose from her place by the fire and returned to the kitchen area. She set the pan on the wooden table. Gwyn followed her, seating herself on one of the wooden chairs.

"He is a heathen, Gwyn. You have said so yourself."

Gwyn's eyes turned serious. "But you could make him believe. If anyone could, it would be you."

Arietta stared at her in surprise. "What makes you think that?"

"There is something about you, Arietta. I do not know what to call it, but it is. . .it is. . .a holy radiance."

Arietta didn't mock what her sister said. She answered seriously, "Did you know that in the holy Scriptures it tells us that *holy* means to be set apart by God?"

Gwyn sat back in her chair slowly. "You have been studying the Scriptures? How is this possible?"

Arietta took one of the loaves of bread they had made this morning and began cutting it into slices. "King Alfred believes that lack of knowledge of the Scriptures is what has brought the Vikings down upon us. Since the people do not know the Scriptures, they are not doing God's will, thus they have brought His wrath upon the country. King Alfred wants everyone to have access to the holy Scriptures."

Gwyn was impressed. "But how did you learn what the Scriptures say? The village does not even have a priest."

"Brother Bertrand at the abbey. He needed help in copying the Scriptures, so he taught some of us to form the letters. At the same time, he told us the meaning of the words we were writing down."

"But I thought even the priests did not know how to read."

Arietta placed the mushrooms on a platter, along with the bread. "That is true, but King Alfred brought scholars from across the sea to teach them."

Gwyn took a mushroom and popped it into her mouth. She studied Arietta as she chewed. "I would like to learn the words of Scripture."

Arietta smiled, her happiness apparent. "I would be glad to teach you."

"I have always remembered the Lord, but I would like to know Him better. Like you."

Wulfric peeked his head around the door. "The meat is ready."

Arietta lifted the platter and followed him out the door. The afternoon sun was waning, and dusk was only a breath away. The fire added light to the darkening landscape; Arietta joined the others huddled around it.

Each man cut a hunk of meat from the roasting pig and ate it suspended on their knives. Their laughter grew louder as the meal progressed, the mead flowing freely from one man to another.

Both Helga and Bjorn sat beside their mother, their heads bobbing with fatigue. Bjorn fought to stay upright, while his sister gave in to the inevitable and laid her head in her mother's lap.

Gwyn and Arietta exchanged smiles. Both rose at the same time. Sidroc rose also, lifting an enquiring brow at his wife.

"Arietta and I will put the children to bed."

Bjorn suddenly sat upright. "Not me," he refuted.

"Yes, you," his father disagreed. The boy would have argued further, but one look from his father brought him to instant silence. He got to his feet with a pout and followed his mother into the cottage.

Arietta took the clay oil lamp from the shelf and lit it with a small tinder from the fire. Holding it by the handle, she led the way into her father's old room.

Gwyn stood looking around, memories of earlier times

reflected by the small smile on her face.

"Why do you not sleep here?" she asked.

Arietta shrugged. "I could not bring myself to do so."

Gwyn nodded understandingly. Arietta took off Helga's clothes, while Gwyn helped her son. "What will you do with the cottage when you and Edwynn marry?"

Arietta pulled back the covers, and the two children climbed beneath. "Sell it, probably."

She tucked the blanket beneath the children's chins and smiled at them, then leaned down to give them each a kiss.

Gwyn smiled mockingly when Bjorn offered no resistance to his aunt's caress. She placed her hands on her hips. "So, you are too old for a mother's kiss, but not an aunt's."

Color flooded the boy's cheeks. He grinned with embarrassment but did not deny it. Gwyn laughed and kissed him anyway. By the time the two adults left the room, both children were asleep.

Gwyn started to return to the others, but Arietta hesitated. She was reluctant to spend more time among the Norsemen, and one in particular. "You go ahead. I have some things to do."

Nodding, Gwyn left her alone.

Arietta decided to leave the others to their revelry, so she opened the front door to the cottage and went outside. Darkness had descended, but the landscape was bathed with moonlight from an almost full moon. She hugged herself, rubbing her arms against the evening's chill.

When Wulfric joined her, she wasn't surprised. It seemed the culmination of the day's events.

"Why did you not return?" he asked quietly.

"I wished to be alone," she answered pointedly.

He ignored the comment. When he moved closer, Arietta hastily stepped away.

Wulfric frowned. "You are afraid of me, but you would face a charging boar?"

Arietta quirked a brow. "If you notice, the boar is now roasting on a spit."

He grinned and again moved closer. Arietta studied his shadowed face, wondering at his intent.

"I would not do the same to you," he assured her in a wickedly amused voice.

Arietta took another step back and found herself against the wall of the cottage. Taking advantage of the opportunity, Wulfric quickly placed his hands on each side of her face. He leaned closer, and Arietta's eyes widened.

"Do you know how a Viking woman shows appreciation for someone saving her life?" His voice was seductively low, and Arietta became alarmed.

Trying to control her panic, she put as much animosity into her voice as she could. "No, I do not." She tried to move away, but his stance was unyielding. She glared into his darkened eyes. "And you did not save me. I saved myself."

His nearness was disturbing. Being used to the men of her country, she did not quite know what to do with this hulking Viking. His slow smile caused the panic to grow. Before he could guess her intentions, she ducked quickly under his arm and moved away from him. The smell of the mead on his breath told her that he just might be uncontrollable.

He followed her slowly. Arietta glanced at the door of the cottage and wondered if she could make it past the Norseman before he could catch her. She would be safe with Gwyn.

Lunging forward, she would have made it, but she tripped over the torn hem of her tunic. Wulfric reacted quickly, reaching out to keep her from falling, pulling her close as he did so. His smile was unnerving.

Though she tried to push away, his hold remained firm and unrelenting. "Wulfric, let me go." The command in her voice was shaky at best.

He grinned, his eyes filled with a teasing light.

Before he could answer, the light from a torch lit their entwined figures. They both turned startled faces to the light. Wulfric frowned at the intruder, but Arietta gave a gasp of recognition. "Edwynn."

four

"Unhand her, Norseman."

Though Edwynn stood at least a head shorter than the Viking, there was menace in his voice and a deadly intensity. Wulfric's arms tensed around Arietta. She shoved against him, trying to put some distance between them.

Ever so slowly, Wulfric released her, his attention now focused on the man standing so close. The torchlight revealed Wulfric's face, and Arietta saw his nostrils flare. Recognizing the Viking's growing anger, she moved between the two men.

"Edwynn, you have returned."

The Saxon's dark-eyed look never wavered from Wulfric. "As you can see."

Arietta was growing more uncomfortable by the minute. The two men stood sizing each other up, and in Arietta's mind, there was no doubt who would come out the victor if there was a fight. Although Edwynn's body was strong and muscled from working the bellows and forge all day, he hadn't the Viking's skill.

"What brings you here so late?" she managed to ask.

For the first time, Edwynn's look turned to her, his possessive gaze shaking her somewhat. "News travels fast in such a small village. I heard that your sister had returned and that she had brought a Viking husband." His look softened. "I wanted to make certain that you were well."

Suddenly a dark shape blocked the lamp light spilling out onto the walkway through the doorway, and Arietta turned to see Gwyn. Her gaze flashed around the small group and returned to Arietta.

Arietta stepped toward her. "This is Edwynn." She turned to her betrothed. "My sister, Gwyn."

Edwynn moved toward them, his eyes glancing briefly at Wulfric, who stood impassively, watching the whole scene.

"I am pleased to meet you. Arietta has told me much of you." When his look rested on Wulfric, his eyes were dark with hostility. "And this is your husband?"

Sensing the tense atmosphere, Gwyn forced a smile. "Wulfric is not my husband but my husband's brother."

The Saxon's eyes darkened further. "I see."

Arietta curled her arm through Edwynn's. She glared defiantly at Wulfric. "Wulfric," she said adamantly. "This is Edwynn. My betrothed."

The Norseman's eyes flickered briefly, and something in them made Arietta's breathing suddenly become more labored. He nodded slightly at Edwynn, then slipped behind Gwyn and returned to the others in the back.

Arietta sighed with relief. She met her sister's look and knew from the frown on her face that there would be questions forthcoming.

"I must return to my husband," Gwyn told them, her look resting on Edwynn briefly. "Perhaps we will see you again on the morrow."

"You can be certain of it," he assured her.

Arietta jerked her glance back to Edwynn, recognizing the hidden anger in his voice. Gwyn nodded briefly, then left.

Arietta looked at Edwynn, her back stiffening. "It was not what it seemed."

Edwynn waited for her to explain. She did so, as briefly as possible. His angry look went past her to the cottage door. "If he molests you again, I will take him before the folkmoot."

To be brought before the village assembly was not something she relished. Knowing it was no idle threat, Arietta patted his arm gently. "I think he will not. Wulfric had too much mead, and tomorrow he will probably regret his actions."

Edwynn's look was skeptical, and she knew that he didn't believe it any more than she did. Deciding to change the subject, she sat down on the stone wall surrounding the cottage.

"Tell me about your trip. How did things go with you?"

Edwynn looked as though he would resist her change of subject, but he settled himself next to her on the wall and proceeded to tell her of his travels.

Arietta watched his face in the light from the open door. His clean-shaven chin held strength, but sometimes she believed that Edwynn's stubbornness about certain things was more vice than virtue. There was no denying he was a handsome man, and many maids in the village had cast their eyes his way, but he had rejected all such advances. He believed he owed Arietta's father, and he would stubbornly cling to his set purpose of marrying her.

She had tried to let him know that, now that her father was dead, she was willing to free him of his betrothal, but his pride would not allow it. She had been hoping and praying that the good Lord would send another woman into his life who might sway him from his intent, but so far, that had not occurred.

After some time, Edwynn took his leave, reminding Arietta that he would see her the next day. Before he left, he pulled her close and pressed his lips against hers in a hard kiss. His eyes roved her face briefly before he picked up his torch and backed slowly away, then quickly disappeared from sight. She watched his disappearing form, her fingers covering her swollen lips, and felt suddenly bewildered. Edwynn had never behaved toward her as he had done tonight. He had seemed almost a stranger.

Reluctantly she entered the cottage but found that the others were still engaged in their feasting and revelry. She hurriedly climbed the ladder to the loft, preparing herself quickly for bed.

When she finally lay beneath the covers, her thoughts kept returning to the time Wulfric had held her in his arms. Though she had resisted him, a part of her had wanted to yield to the strength and security she felt in his arms. Edwynn's kiss had left her unmoved, and now she tried vainly to keep her mind from picturing herself instead in Wulfric's arms.

She made a sound of frustration in her throat, biting her knuckle with unintentional zeal. More confused than ever, she rolled over and forced herself to sleep.

જ

Wulfric stood at the side of the cottage, watching the Saxon retreat down the road. Even after Edwynn's torch had disappeared, he continued to stand there. His eyes lifted to the loft window. He could see Arietta's shadow moving about in the semidark, and for a brief instant, he thought of going to her.

A light touch on his arm brought his gaze downward. Gwyn stood beside him, her own look going to the loft window. "She is not like the women you are used to, Wulfric. Have a care."

Gwyn certainly was right about that. Arietta was nothing like any woman he had ever encountered, and he wanted her for his own. Like so many of his kind, he was used to taking, but now he knew he had to find a different way. He realized that Arietta would fight him every inch of the way, and although he knew without conceit that he would arise the victor of such a confrontation, he wanted Arietta to come to him willingly. Innocence shone from her beautiful green eyes, and he must respect that purity. If nothing else, Arietta's God would demand it.

Wulfric caught his sister-in-law's look and smiled wryly. There was a warning in her eyes, those eyes that were so like Arietta's. Feeling somehow rebuked for his earlier thoughts, he watched her go past him and enter the cottage.

When Wulfric returned to the men, he found them preparing to leave. Ingvar lifted heavy eyes to Wulfric, his head bobbing from side to side. "When will you be ready to leave for Iceland?" he demanded in a slurred voice.

Wulfric frowned. "I have told you. When the others are settled."

The other man's eyes darkened. "What is that to us? They have chosen to turn their back on their people and become

English. They choose to worship a foreign God. Let their foreign God take care of them."

Wulfric's eyes grew cold and stormy. "I will not abandon my family until I know that they are taken care of. Whether they choose to worship Thor or this other Christ is of no concern to me. They are my family, and here I will stay until *I* say I am ready to leave."

Ingvar stepped forward, clenching his hands into fists at his side, but something in Wulfric's eyes made him hesitate. Wulfric was well known among the people for his strength and power. Slowly uncurling his hands, Ingvar gave his head a quick affirmative jerk. "As you wish." Pushing by Wulfric, Ingvar took his leave, closely followed by Godfred.

Sidroc eyed his brother uneasily. "I am pleased that you are staying, Wulfric. I had hoped that you would make your home among us here."

Wulfric's enigmatic gaze met Sidroc's. "I will stay as long as I can, but I will not be baptized and accept this foreign God."

Sidroc clapped a hand on his brother's shoulder. "I understand, but if *I* cannot convince you to stay, perhaps someone else can." He looked up at the loft window.

Wulfric smiled slowly but said nothing.

❧

The next morning, Gwyn helped Arietta to set the bread for the day. She watched Arietta closely, and Arietta grew uncomfortable under her steady regard.

"What is it you wish to say?" Arietta finally asked in exasperation.

Gwyn looked at Arietta, her eyes hard. "Arietta, do not trifle with a man like Wulfric."

Filled with sudden rage, Arietta turned on her sister. "Trifle with him! I have done everything that I can to stay out of his way."

Gwyn sighed, rubbing her face with one hand. She finally regarded her sister soberly. "I believe Wulfric is enamored of you."

Arietta's mouth dropped open. She wasn't quite certain what to say to such a declaration. Her sister had to be insane. What was there about her to attract such a man? She was plain by even her own countrymen's standards, but among the Vikings, she would surely be considered a weakling. "Why would you think such a preposterous thing?"

Gwyn's mouth twitched into a reluctant smile. She took Arietta by the shoulders, looking into her eyes intensely. "You have no idea how people really see you, Beloved. Even after only a few days back among the people, I see their regard of you."

Arietta snorted softly. "Old people and children."

Gwyn's smile transformed into a full-fledged grin. She shook her head in vexation. "There has never been conceit in you. Even as a child, you underestimated your own influence. Remember the ealdorman who had to judge Galdon for thievery?"

Arietta remembered. Though her father and Gwyn had been appalled, Arietta as a child of five had stepped boldly into the assembly of the folkmoot and proclaimed the man's innocence. It took at least two witnesses on someone's behalf, but after hearing her statement, the ealdorman had judged Galdon innocent. Arietta's penchant for telling the truth had justified the man in the ealdorman's eyes.

Gwyn lifted the bread from the table and exited the back door. Arietta followed her, knowing there was more that her sister wanted to say.

Gwyn knelt before the oven, looking over her shoulder at Arietta. Her eyes were serious. "Just be careful around Wulfric."

Arietta lifted one eyebrow. "I assure you, I had no intention of doing otherwise."

Satisfied, Gwyn smiled. "Good. I know I am intruding into affairs that are not my own, but I love you and would not see you hurt."

Arietta knelt beside her, taking her hand with one of her

own. "My business *is* your business. I will listen to what you have to say anytime."

They exchanged smiles, then hugs. Arietta's head rested briefly on her sister's shoulder, and she felt truly thankful that God had seen fit to bring her sister back into her life.

After they finished their chores, Gwyn suggested that they go and watch the men beach the ship. They followed a much-used path through the woods and came out on the edge of the river.

Sidroc saw them first, lifting his hand in a silent wave. Wulfric noticed the movement and followed the direction of his brother's look. He quickly turned away when he saw them standing there.

Gwyn grinned saucily. " He will never admit it, but I believe Wulfric is embarrassed about last night."

Arietta's eyes took on fire. "He should be."

They did not hear anyone approach until another woman hailed them. Gwyn's smile turned into a grimace. "Wendella," she told Arietta through clenched teeth.

Arietta's eyes widened in surprise at her sister's hostile tone. She turned to watch the other woman as she came closer. Arietta felt her stomach clench with instant envy. Wendella had the long, silver blond hair of her kind. Her features were perfect, her cheekbones high, her skin a flawless gold.

Wendella's frosty blue eyes fastened on Arietta, then dismissed her as not worthy of attention. She spoke to Gwyn in Norse, and Gwyn answered her in the same tongue. Both feigned friendship, though it was easy to see that their cordiality was a farce.

The woman turned her gaze on Wulfric, her eyes hungry with desire. Her slow smile made Arietta's chest suddenly tighten with an unfamiliar feeling.

Wendella strode down to the ship, her tinkling laugh ringing back to Gwyn and Arietta still standing at the edge of the forest.

"Be careful of Wendella, Arietta. If she finds out that

Wulfric is interested in you, there is no telling what she might do."

Arietta watched the other woman boldly flirt with Wulfric. "She is very beautiful."

Gwyn nodded, albeit reluctantly. "And she knows it. The only men who have been able to resist her wiles are my Sidroc and Wulfric, and I do not know how much longer Wulfric will continue to ignore her."

Arietta's eyes grew large. "She went after Sidroc?"

The darkness of Gwyn's eyes spoke of hidden anger. "Yes, but she failed. Unfortunately for her, I knew that Sidroc loved me. I had faith in him, believed him when he told me he was innocent."

Arietta frowned. "I do not understand. If she had so many conquests, why did she want Sidroc?"

Gwyn flashed her sister an exasperated look. "You are so innocent." She turned to contemplate her husband, and her eyes softened immeasurably. "Sidroc was a challenge. It was a matter of pride."

Arietta noticed Wendella place a hand on Wulfric's bulging biceps as he hoisted the front end of the ship onto a roller. She felt her insides tighten again and wondered at her reaction. Surely she wasn't jealous.

Ingvar joined Wulfric, while Sidroc pushed on one side, Godfred on the other. The ship slid up the rollers and was quickly moved ashore to be made ready for whenever it was needed again.

"Wendella is Godfred's sister," Gwyn explained.

Arietta studied the other man and saw a resemblance. Both had hair the color of the moonlight. Had Godfred a clean-shaven face, he would no doubt be as handsome as his sister was beautiful.

A young boy passed by them, startling them out of their pre-occupation with the scene below. He smiled shyly at Arietta and more boldly at Gwyn. She returned his smile with the same look she reserved for her children. "That is Olaf," she said to Arietta after he had passed. "He is Wendella's thrall."

Watching the young man, Arietta frowned. "Thrall?"

"Slave."

Dismayed, Arietta once again watched the young man. He bowed deferentially to Wendella, speaking with his look cast to the ground. Not liking what he had to say, Wendella's face darkened with fury, and raising her hand, she struck the boy across the face. He staggered back, keeping his look firmly fixed on the ground.

Roused to fury, Arietta bounded down the small hill and drew abreast of Olaf. Taking the boy's chin in her hand, she gently lifted his face to meet her look. Red fingerprints were blazoned across his cheek.

Eyes darkening further, Arietta whirled to face Wendella. "What kind of woman are you?" she hissed with unbridled wrath.

Startled, Wendella took a hasty step back. Gwyn joined them, taking Arietta by the arm. "Arietta, you will only make matters worse."

Wendella quickly recovered from her surprise. She glared at Arietta. "What is the matter with you?"

Arietta pointed to Olaf. "He is only a boy. How dare you strike him that way."

Wendella came closer until they were face to face. "He is *my* thrall. I will do with him whatever I please."

The rise and fall of Arietta's chest was the only visible indication of her growing anger. "That is not the way to treat a child. It is not the Christian thing to do."

Wendella glared at Arietta, then spat on the ground. "Neither am I a Christian. I have no time for your weak God." Her voice became more threatening. "And you would do well to mind your own business."

Arietta unleashed the full power of her wrath on the other woman, lifting her hand and striking the woman with a resounding smack across the face.

Startled, Wendella lifted her hand to her reddening cheek.

Her face contorted with rage. "Why you. . ."

No one had noticed Wulfric move, but suddenly, he stood behind Wendella and wrapped his arms around her. She struggled ineffectively against his hold, her teeth gnashing with fury.

Arietta stood before them, appalled by her actions. The anger drained from her, and she hung her head in shame. She had never understood why others abused children, but to take her anger out on another was uncalled for and ungodly. She lifted anguished eyes to Wendella. "I beg your forgiveness. I do not know what came over me."

"You will beg for more than forgiveness if I ever get hold of you," Wendella snarled in return.

Arietta lifted her eyes to meet Wulfric's. He was watching her intently, but she couldn't read what was in his eyes. "Please let her go."

His blond brows winged upward. "She will kill you."

"Maybe so, but please let her go."

Wendella stopped struggling, her look fastening on Arietta's contrite form. Recognizing the sincerity of the apology, some of the anger left her eyes.

Wulfric slowly released her, and Wendella shook herself free from his restraint. She came to Arietta and stood before her, her rage still evident. She lifted her hand to strike Arietta across the face, but when Arietta stood resolutely before her, she slowly lowered her hand. "Have you no pride?" Wendella asked in disbelief.

"The Scriptures teach us that pride goeth before destruction." Arietta lifted honest eyes to Wendella's puzzled ones. "I am truly sorry for striking you. I beg you to forgive me."

Wendella looked at the group standing around. She regarded Arietta with scorn. "Your God makes you weak." Turning, she strode away. They watched her go in silence.

After a long moment, Sidroc met his wife's look. "Why not take Arietta and go home now," he suggested.

Arietta needed no further bidding. All she wanted to do was go someplace and hide. Her face burned with shame, the whole scene playing itself out over and over in her mind. Since the Norsemen had entered their lives, she'd seemed to be transforming into one of them herself, her emotions cascading from one extreme to the other. Where was her restraint? It was not like her to act so wildly. She needed to go somewhere alone to pray for forgiveness and for help to control her actions.

Gwyn walked by her side saying nothing. When they reached the turn to the village, Arietta stopped. "You go on. There's something that I need to do."

Gwyn lifted a questioning brow. "You are going to the cave?"

Arietta nodded, still unable to look her sister in the face.

Gwyn's hand fastened on her forearm. "Listen to me, Arietta. She had it coming to her."

Lifting chastened eyes to her sister's, Arietta shook her head. "Not by me. I am not her judge. Only God has the power to judge someone's actions."

Gwyn gave her a half-smile. "I understand how you feel, but truly you did nothing seriously wrong."

"Did I not? What will Wendella think of my God now? What kind of Christian woman will she see me as?"

"More than likely, a *Viking* one," Gwyn answered caustically. "When the daughter of a chieftain, she was rather spoiled. No one has ever stood up to her before."

"You spoke in the past," Arietta responded. "Is she no longer a chieftain's daughter?"

Gwyn shook her head. "No. Two chieftains fought, and her father lost. In Norway, there are too many people for the little land available. That is why we have come back here and why the others will travel on to Iceland."

Arietta rested her hands on her sister's uneasy shoulders. "Whatever the reason, I am glad to have you back."

Gwyn smiled reassuringly. "I somehow doubt that Wendella will bother you again."

Arietta's shook her head. "I saw her eyes, Gwyn. I have made a terrible enemy."

five

A few weeks later, Arietta walked beside Edwynn, a frown forming on her face. She stopped suddenly, facing him with her hands on her hips, her green eyes sparking with anger. "Edwynn, why are you so against helping others? Aren't we supposed to help each other? Is not that the Christian thing to do? Even Brother Bertrand says so."

He blinked his dark eyes at her, his brows forming to make a mirror image of her own. A sparrow flew to the path in front of them, tilted his head slightly in their direction, then quickly flew to a nearby tree.

"It is one thing to help others when they have no other option," Edwynn replied, "but it is foolish to help Martha when it was through her own son's foolishness that she is in need."

Arietta felt her anger begin to rise. She crossed her arms over her chest, clutching her forearms with her hands to keep from striking out at Edwynn's arrogance. "So because Asimund was foolish enough to fall from a tree, his family should starve?"

Obviously realizing his mistake, Edwynn's voice became more placating. The grime from the forge was imbedded in the hand that he held out to her. "The boy is forever into mischief. If you step in to help them out whenever things go wrong because of his foolishness, he will never learn to take responsibility for his actions."

Arietta ignored the outstretched hand. In a way, Edwynn was right, but Arietta knew Asimund well enough to know that he was suffering right along with his family. The boy had matured quickly over the last few months. "Asimund has learned his lesson. I do not think the boy will again endanger himself so foolishly when he knows how much his family depends on him."

Edwynn looked at her for a long moment, then sighed heavily. He shifted the sack he carried to his other hand. "Very well, let us go to Martha's and take them your sustenance. But with five extra mouths to feed, I do not see how you can continue to be so generous."

Arietta turned and started back along the path, her brown wool dress swishing with the movement. Though she was still aggravated with him, she allowed Edwynn to take her hand. "Sidroc and Wulfric have done well keeping us supplied with meat, and my dried vegetables have yet to run out. Even Bjorn seems to be a born fisherman."

"There was a time when *I* supplied your needs," Edwynn answered darkly.

For the first time, Arietta recognized the jealousy in Edwynn's voice. She glanced at him, noting the set jaw. "And how was that any different from me helping to supply Martha's needs?" she asked him softly.

Edwynn pulled her to a sudden stop, his dark eyes flashing angrily. "Because you are going to marry me."

Arietta met his look unflinchingly. "But I am not your wife yet."

His lips tightened into a straight line. "What are you saying? That you no longer wish to marry me?"

"I am not saying that at all. What I am saying is that you helped me even though we are no relation. It is what I am trying to do for Martha and her family."

Edwynn shook his head in exasperation. "It is not the same thing at all, but I can see that we will never agree on this. Let us finish this mission of mercy. Then we can discuss our wedding."

Arietta quickly averted her eyes. She turned and continued on her way, her stomach suddenly coiled into a tight knot. Her wedding was the last thing she wished to discuss, but she could tell by the inflexible quality of Edwynn's voice that he would be put off no longer.

When they reached Martha's small hut, they found the two

youngest children outside playing. Their screams of laughter brought a quick smile to Arietta's face. When the children noticed Arietta and Edwynn, they instantly hushed, their large, dark eyes staring at the two solemnly.

Arietta smiled reassuringly and stepped forward. "Judith, Bertin, where is your mother?"

Bertin snaked out an arm, pointing toward the interior of the hut. Arietta went in the direction indicated, tousling Bertin's hair as she went by him. He frowned, ducking away from her touch, causing Judith to giggle at his annoyance.

"I will wait here," Edwynn told her, handing over the bag of provisions. Taking the bag from him, Arietta nodded and turned to go inside.

The darkened hut was cold, the embers of the fire pit long extinguished. Martha, looking out the small window aperture at the forest beyond, turned when Arietta entered. Her frayed dress was mended in several places, as was her *cyrtel*, but both were scrupulously clean.

The woman's weary face lit with her smile of welcome. "Arietta, welcome."

Arietta's eyes settled on Asimund, lying on the small bed in the corner. He watched her unblinkingly, his mouth turned down at the corners. Arietta included him in her smile. "Hello, Asimund. Are you better today?"

The boy's eyes fastened on his right leg, bound between two sticks. He lifted his gaze to Arietta. "I am well enough to care for my family now."

His brooding look focused on her bag of supplies. She handed them to Martha and went to sit next to Asimund. He allowed her to brush his dark hair back from his forehead as she said, "I am certain that you are, but your mother just wants to make certain that no further harm comes to you until you heal completely. You are the man of the house, and she needs you."

He did not say anything for a moment, then his mouth turned up into a cheeky grin. "What did you bring today?"

Arietta smiled her relief. "I brought some honey cakes, along with some berry jelly."

A bright light entered his eyes, and he turned his pleading look on his mother. "May I have some, Mother?"

Martha gave him a half-hearted smile. "Of course."

While Asimund ate his treat, Arietta pulled Martha to the side. "Your fire has gone out. I will bring you some more." Martha thanked her politely, but Arietta could see that there was much on the woman's mind. She studied the woman's tired face. "Do not worry, Martha. God will provide."

Martha snorted slightly, not able to hold Arietta's look. "And you."

Arietta sat uninvited at the woman's small table. Martha reluctantly took the seat across from her. The woman was trying her best to hide her concern, but she was failing miserably. Arietta could see how Martha's pride wanted to refuse the help she was receiving, but her love for her family made it necessary.

"I learned many Bible stories when I was helping Brother Bertrand copy the Scriptures," Arietta began slowly, noting Martha's increased attention. "Did you know that long ago, in the early church, people sold their possessions to help their brother and sister Christians?"

Martha leaned forward, her look intense. "Truly?"

Arietta nodded. "Yes, and they were blessed because of it." She leaned over the table and placed her hand on Martha's rough, work-hardened one. "Martha," she asked softly. "Would you not do the same for me if I were in need?"

The woman nodded slightly. She caught Arietta's knowing eye, and her shoulders slumped with defeat. "You are right, Arietta. I apologize for my lack of thankfulness."

Arietta smiled and stood up. "The apology is not necessary, but I will accept it anyway." She emptied the sack on the table, clutching it in her hands. "Remember, Martha. Too much pride is a sin."

Martha nodded. "I will remember. Thank you again."

"I must go. Edwynn is waiting for me." She placed her hand on Martha's shoulder. "If there is anything that you need, please let me know."

Martha cast her gaze to the floor. "You have done so much already."

"It has pleased me to do so."

Arietta had a hard time holding back her own tears when Martha's swimming eyes met hers. It must be hard, having known the love and care of a husband, to suddenly be without that man. She hugged the other woman, then hurriedly left the hut. When she passed Bertin and Judith, she threw them a smile. "Your mother has a treat for you inside."

They needed no other bidding. Throwing down their sticks, they raced inside.

Edwynn frowned after them. "Not even so much as a thank you."

Arietta refrained from saying anything. Edwynn walked beside her in silence for some time before he put out an arm to stop her. He motioned to a fallen log on the side of the path. "Let us sit here for a moment."

Arietta knew what was coming, and her heart started to beat with trepidation. She sat on the log, her attention focused on some ants scurrying across the path.

Edwynn cleared his throat, seating himself next to her. "Arietta, we must set a date for our wedding. You cannot possibly continue to live in your house with. . .with so many others."

Arietta sighed, then lifted her head reluctantly until she was able to see Edwynn's earnest face next to hers. "Edwynn, please understand. I have only had my sister back in my life for a few weeks. I want to spend some time with her and my niece and nephew."

His lips thinned with displeasure. "You can marry me and still be able to spend time with your sister."

That was certainly true enough, but Arietta was hesitant to agree to anything concerning a marriage that she no longer wished to consummate. She studied Edwynn quietly, uncertain as to her reasons for feeling so adamant about refusing. She truly did not wish to hurt Edwynn when he had been so good to her.

"Edwynn," she pleaded softly. "I need more time."

His eyes suddenly hardened. "As per the agreement, we will be wed in two weeks, on your twenty-first birthday." He got swiftly to his feet, glaring down at her. "That is my final decision."

He strode off, leaving Arietta fighting mingled feelings of anger and fear. Since the marriage had been agreed upon by her father and Edwynn in the sight of Brother Bertrand, she really had no choice.

Getting slowly to her feet, she pondered whether to return to the village or go somewhere else and try to work through this problem. Setting her lips firmly, she turned back the way she had just traversed and made her way through the woods to Old Wiglaf's house.

The old man had lived alone for some years, quietly tending to his own business. Arietta considered him a far more godly man than Brother Bertrand. Whereas Brother Bertrand taught and studied the Scriptures, Wiglaf actually lived them. Arietta wondered how the old man could live his life so much in the will of God's commands when the old man had never learned the Scriptures except for those that Arietta had been able to share with him. Wiglaf just seemed to live a godly life instinctively, helping others whenever he could.

Now the old man was failing in health, and Arietta worried that soon he would no longer be able to take care of himself. She had taken to delivering Wiglaf various odds and ends whenever she visited Martha, spending as much time as she could with him. Today, she had nothing to bring but herself, but she knew that with Wiglaf, it would be enough.

Although she could feel the chill of the late autumn air, Wiglaf's door stood open. As she approached, a lone squirrel hurried out the open doorway and disappeared up a nearby tree. She smiled. Even the animals loved Old Wiglaf and knew that the man was too gentle to harm them. Though he would eat meat if it was brought to him, he couldn't bring himself to kill any animal but the fish in the streams.

Arietta peeked her head in the door, stopping in stunned surprise when not only Wiglaf turned his head her way, but Wulfric as well.

Wiglaf's face brightened at her sudden appearance. "Come in. Come in, Arietta."

Arietta hesitated, her eyes caught by Wulfric's penetrating gaze. "I did not mean to intrude. You have other company. I will return another time."

She started to move away, but Wiglaf's croaky voice stopped her. "No, no." He waved her forward. "Come inside, Child. Come and meet my friend, Wulfric."

Wulfric's lips tilted into that slow smile that so devastated her thinking processes. "We have already met," he told the older man, his deep voice giving away nothing of his amusement.

Wiglaf looked surprised, his glance going from one to the other. "Have you? Well then, come in, Arietta, and join us. We are not strangers here."

Arietta slowly entered the hut, noticing Wulfric's lips twitch with amusement at her evident reluctance. Setting her chin determinedly, she made her way to Wiglaf's side. It was only then that she noticed the game board between them. Curious, she moved closer. "What are you playing? I do not recognize the game."

Wiglaf smiled. "It is called *hnefatafl.* Wulfric is teaching me."

Arietta looked at Wulfric suspiciously. "The game is yours?"

One side of his mouth curved up into a sly smile. "It is. I would be glad to teach you as well."

Arietta recognized the provocation in his voice. She lowered her lids so that he could not see the gleam that entered her eyes. "Perhaps later. Right now, you two go on with your game. I will just watch."

The two men nodded to her, then turned their attention back to the board. Within seconds, both men had forgotten her presence. Arietta sat quietly watching each man and familiarizing herself with the moves they were making.

Before long, Wiglaf's king was surrounded by four of Wulfric's pieces. He looked at the Norseman, smiling wryly. "It would seem you have beaten me again, Wulfric."

Wulfric's eyes twinkled. "But it took me a lot longer to do so this time, Wiglaf. You have learned the game well, and it will be a hard chore for me to beat you in the future."

Wiglaf clutched a piece in his hand, lifting it toward Wulfric. "Next time, my friend. Next time."

Amazed at their camaraderie, Arietta could only stare from one to the other. As though becoming aware of her presence for the first time, Wulfric tilted his head at her in question.

Arietta ignored him. Turning to the old man, she smiled prettily. "I am sorry, Wiglaf, but I have not brought you anything this time. I am afraid my mind was elsewhere."

Wiglaf waved away her apology. "No matter, Arietta. Wulfric keeps me well supplied."

Color stole into the Norseman's cheeks at Arietta's astounded look. He rose quickly. "I am afraid I must leave you now, Wiglaf. I will try to come again in a few days, so be prepared to lose again."

Wiglaf chuckled at the challenge. "We shall see, Wulfric. We shall see. I may be feeble in body, but here. . ." He tapped his left temple with a finger. "I am as strong as ever."

When Wiglaf started to rise, Wulfric lay a hand on his shoulder. "Be still. I can see my own way out."

Arietta surprised herself by saying, "I will come with you." She could read the objection forming in his eyes and smiled hastily at Wiglaf. "I will return on the morrow."

The old man's eyes went from Arietta to Wulfric. His smile became almost mischievous. "Do that, Arietta. I will be waiting for you."

Arietta had to hurry to catch up with Wulfric, who had already started down the path to the village. She drew up beside him, taking two steps to his one. Seeing her problem, he slowed his stride.

He answered her question before she could even ask it. "I met Wiglaf when I was out hunting one day."

Arietta shuffled the thoughts in her head, trying to put them into the proper order for the questions she wanted to ask. "He is a wonderful old man. Everyone loves him."

Wulfric's voice was soft when he answered. "He reminds me of my grandfather."

Surprised, Arietta turned to him. "You have a grandfather?"

He looked down at her briefly. "Had. He is in Valhalla."

Arietta felt saddened by the news. If Wulfric's grandfather was anything like Wiglaf, she hated to think that the man would spend eternity separated from God due to his lack of knowledge of the Lord Jesus Christ.

Wulfric looked at her again. "You would say he was in heaven. He accepted your Christ when the priest came to our homeland, but he was also a great warrior."

The tenderness in his voice touched Arietta deeply. All she had ever seen from this man was his intense, passionate nature. It had never occurred to her that there might be a softer side to him.

When the brush thickened around them, they had to walk one in front of the other. Wulfric held branches aside for her to pass, and she was touched by his chivalry.

"Why did you not let Wiglaf win?" Arietta asked him curiously.

Wulfric jerked his look back to her, one eyebrow lifted in scorn. "When he wins, he will know that he has won fairly."

"But surely, it would not hurt to let him win sometimes."

Wulfric stopped in his tracks, his hands placed firmly on his hips. His look was scathing. "A man does not need such artifices."

Arietta stopped with him. She placed her hands on her hips

in like posture, glaring up at him. "If someone continues to lose, they will soon grow discouraged and give up."

"I have not seen it so. Losing only makes one more determined to win."

"Maybe for someone like you!"

Before she knew what was happening, he dropped his ever present ax to the ground, reached out, grabbed her by the forearms, and pulled her closer. "What do you mean, someone like me?"

She swallowed hard at the dark look on his face. She pushed her palms against his chest, trying to act braver than she felt. "You like to conquer," she answered, her voice quavering. "It is in your nature."

His eyes moved over her face slowly, before meshing with her green ones. "What do you know about me, Arietta? What do you *really* know about me?"

She was surprised at the hurt in his voice. She stared back at him, perplexed. "I. . .I do not know anything, really."

He released her, and she rubbed her arms with her hands. Though he hadn't hurt her, her skin still tingled where he had touched her.

He turned and started forward again. Arietta followed. She glanced at his rigid back, wishing she could have stilled her wayward tongue. "Do you let no one win? Not even Bjorn?"

"No, not even Bjorn."

Arietta frowned. "But he is just a child."

Wulfric stopped and turned to her again. The suddenness of it caught Arietta by surprise, and she rammed into his rock solid chest. He reached out his hands to keep her upright, releasing her immediately.

"Someday Bjorn will be a man," he explained in a tightly controlled voice. "He must learn that what he gains, he gains by his own initiative, not because someone gives it to him because they feel sorry for him. From the day he is born, a man-child is just that—a man. He needs to be molded and made strong to withstand this harsh life."

Arietta's mouth tightened at his declaration. She would never understand the ways of his people. "And if he gives up?" she asked.

Wulfric's lips curled slowly. "He will not. He is a Norseman."

Arietta sighed, rolling her eyes heavenward. She placed her hands on her hips, glaring at him. "But Wiglaf is not. He is old and not as capable as he once was."

Wulfric's stance was unyielding. He crossed his arms over his chest, returning her glare. "When Bjorn and Wiglaf beat me at *hnefatafl*, they will *know* they have won. It will be a great victory for them. Not one that can be taken away by someone suggesting that I have let them win."

Arietta gulped a deep breath and gave him a look of sheer frustration. "Has no one ever beaten you?"

"Yes, many times."

She smiled. "Will you teach me, then?"

"I will be more than happy to vanquish you," he suggested softly.

six

After her first encounter with Wulfric at Old Wiglaf's, Arietta frequently found the two men together. At first it had been unnerving, especially after Wulfric's declaration, but then she began to see a different side of the man, a side she hadn't known existed.

Always before she had been as terrified of the Norsemen as anyone else in England, but having lived among them for the past several weeks, her fears had rapidly diminished. They were no different from any other humans, with just as many needs and wants. The fact that they had a violent past caused many to fear them, but Arietta had grown accustomed to their arrogant and fierce ways.

Sidroc and Wulfric spent many weeks building, but finally the day arrived when Gwyn's new home was ready. Arietta had mixed feelings about the move. Though she was happy for her sister, she would miss her daily presence sorely. Gwyn had offered for Arietta to sell her own house and move in with them, but Arietta was reluctant. She had been on her own for so long, she did not think it would sit well with her to be under another man's roof, no matter how large. Sidroc and Wulfric had spent much time preparing it, and instead of one long house where the whole family would live together, they had divided it into several different rooms.

Gwyn's eyes glowed as she walked along to her new home, chatting feverishly with Arietta. Both of their arms were loaded with goods that Sidroc had brought with them from Norway. Bjorn followed along in their footsteps, leading a ram and two ewes, the beginning of Sidroc's new herd.

A sharp scream brought them to a sudden halt. Arietta whirled to find Helga cowering on the forest floor, arms covering her head, and a goat standing over her. Arietta couldn't help it. She laughed, and Gwyn joined in.

"Get up, Helga," Gwyn commanded firmly. "You must not allow the goat to see that you are afraid of her."

Bjorn frowned at his sister in disgust. "Afraid of a goat!"

Helga lifted tear-drenched eyes to her brother, glaring at him defiantly. "She bit me!"

Ever at a fault before a child's tears, Arietta dropped her supplies and knelt beside Helga. She shoved the goat away and gently lifted the child to her feet, brushing down her clothes as she did so. "Where did she bite you?"

Helga lifted a red finger toward her aunt. Her swimming blue eyes asked for sympathy, and Arietta was quick to respond. Taking the finger, she gently wiped away the dirt and the small trickle of blood, then raised it to her own lips to give it a kiss. Her eyes met her niece's, and she smiled. "Better?"

The child nodded, giving a final sniff. Arietta picked up her load, then took Helga by the hand. "Come, Helga. Since Bjorn is so brave and such a strong boy, we will let him take the goat as well as the sheep."

Arietta's twinkling eyes met her sister's, and she closed one eye in a wink. Gwyn's lips tugged into a smile. "I agree. Here, Bjorn."

Bjorn reluctantly took the proffered leash. He looked from one to the other, stiffening his back at his sister's thrust-out tongue.

When they finally reached the house, Sidroc and Wulfric were busy building a pen. Sidroc smiled at his wife. "Well, Wife. What do you think?"

Her sparkling eyes spoke for her, but she answered him, nonetheless. "It is wonderful, Sidroc. You and Wulfric have worked hard."

Sidroc glanced at his brother askance. "So now Wulfric is free to travel on to Iceland."

Wulfric's look clashed with Arietta's. She glanced quickly away.

"I am afraid that will have to wait until spring," he said. "The seas will be too rough right now."

Sidroc took the leads of the sheep and maneuvered them into the pen. He eyed his brother skeptically. "I think Ingvar will not be too happy with that news."

Arietta smiled at Gwyn. "I will miss you."

Gwyn took both of her hands, clutching them tightly. "We are not far. We will see each other every day."

Arietta knew that was probably true, but still, things would be different. She had grown accustomed to her sister's family about her small house. She would miss the children's laughter and Sidroc's gentle teasing.

And Wulfric? Would she miss Wulfric? Though she tried to deny it, something told her that she would. It was odd, but she felt more alive in his presence than at any other time.

The underbrush rattled, and Wendella came gliding out from the forest. She glanced at each one, but her baleful look rested longest on Arietta. She turned her attention to Wulfric. "We heard that Sidroc was finished with his house. Does this mean that we will be leaving for Iceland soon?"

Sidroc and Wulfric exchanged glances. Gwyn lifted one eyebrow, inclining her head to the side. "Hello, Wendella."

Wendella's face colored, and she looked apologetic. "I beg excuse, Gwyn. I did not mean to overlook you. Greetings." She smiled at Bjorn and Helga. "And to you too." The smile froze on her face when she turned to Arietta. "And to you."

Although Arietta distrusted the Norsewoman, she truly wished to make amends for her earlier treatment of her. She smiled and held out a hand. "Come see the house, Wendella. Sidroc and Wulfric have done a wonderful job."

Surprise flashed through Wendella's eyes. Though she did not take the offered hand, she moved to join them by the door of the house. Her look was veiled when it rested on Arietta, but she smiled at Gwyn. Gwyn looked from one to the other doubtfully, then preceded them inside.

The house was far larger than Arietta's, though her house

was considered by many to be rather grand since it had more than one room. Sidroc had built this house with an eye to having privacy. In the center of the main room was the fire pit, with benches built into the walls around it. Off to one side was a separate kitchen area, and beyond that two other rooms. The daub-and-wattle walls still smelled of the fresh mud used to supply them, and Sidroc had chosen to use a shingle roof rather than one of thatch. Arietta had to admit she was impressed with all the hard work that had gone into its construction.

When they exited the house, Sidroc awaited their reaction.

"It is a wonderful house," Arietta was quick to assure him.

Gwyn smiled at her husband, and it was obvious that hers was the only reaction he was really interested in. "I love it, Sidroc. You and Wulfric have done well."

Sidroc shrugged, clearly pleased by the praise. "I could not have done it without Wulfric."

Wendella crossed to Wulfric's side, her teeth flashing brightly in a sly smile. "Wulfric can do anything."

Arietta's brows drew down into a frown, but when she caught Wulfric's defiant grin, she quickly turned away. She handed Gwyn the last basket she had been clutching, smiling half-heartedly. "I must go now. I promised Edwynn that I would help him with a few things."

Gwyn looked as though she wanted to say something, but a warning glance from her husband silenced her. She took the basket and hugged Arietta at the same time. "You will come later?"

Arietta nodded, her look grazing each of them. She smiled at Helga, and the girl smiled back. When she turned to leave, she found Wulfric's gaze fastened on her. He said nothing, but she could feel him watching her until she disappeared into the forest.

Wulfric waited until she was well on the way before he turned to the others. "I will see that she gets there safely." He ignored Wendella's glowering frown as he picked up his ax and followed after Arietta.

It did not take him long to catch up with her. She turned to him in surprise, lifting an eloquent eyebrow. "Did you wish something?"

His supercilious look made her grind her teeth together. "I was going to the village. I thought I might as well go with you and keep you safe."

She gave him a frosty look. "And am I safe with *you?*"

He grinned but said nothing.

"I thought not," she told him in vexation.

Arietta was trying to decide how to voice the question that had been plaguing her for some time. She knew that Wulfric wouldn't hesitate to tell her to mind her own business, but she was thoroughly curious. "Wulfric, is it you who has been supplying Martha with food?"

He continued striding along beside her. "Why do you ask?"

"Because her son said that he saw a huge Viking drop a sack beside their house. That sack contained fresh game. Was it you?"

He shrugged.

"And was it you who has done the same for several others in the village?"

Arietta laid a hand on his arm, causing him to stop. He avoided looking into her eyes, but when he finally did, she could see uncertainty.

"Thank you." It was all she said, but it was enough. His shoulders relaxed, and they moved on.

They traveled some way in silence before Wulfric reached out a hand, pulling her to a stop. His eyes were unusually serious. "Edwynn is not the man for you."

Surprised, Arietta could only stare. She loosened his hold from her arm and pushed him away with unnecessary force. "That is not for you to say."

His look darkened considerably at her physical rejection. Before she could ascertain his intentions, he grabbed her by the forearms, pulling her close. She did not resist him, except to glare into his icy blue eyes.

"You need a man to keep you warm on long winter nights," he murmured roughly.

She lifted a brow, tilting her head arrogantly. "I have a man who will do so."

Wulfric drew in a jagged breath. He pulled her closer, studying her face, and Arietta thought it time to put a stop to this odd conversation. She tried to free herself from his hold, but once again his superior strength had its way.

Wulfric dropped his lips to hers, and suddenly the whole world receded into nothingness. Arietta struggled against him briefly, but she couldn't deny the intense feelings engendered by his kiss. Her struggles lessened, then ceased altogether, until she was returning his kiss with a fervor she hadn't realized she possessed.

When Wulfric finally pulled back from her, his eyes had darkened with his feelings. "You need a man," he told her huskily, "who will make your blood sing when he kisses you."

Arietta took several deep, steadying breaths. When she pushed against him, he released her instantly.

"I am not an animal, Wulfric. God gave me the ability to use my own mind, and He would expect me to keep my promises," she told him, appalled by her unexpected response to his kiss.

His countenance darkened with anger. "You would marry a man knowing that you have feelings for another man."

"I never said that I had feelings for you."

"You did not need to," he returned softly. "Your lips did it for you."

Arietta felt that she was fast losing this argument. One thing she had learned about Wulfric: He could be ruthless whenever he wanted something. She suddenly, inexplicably feared for Edwynn.

"In two weeks I will be wed to Edwynn," she told him inflexibly. "That is my decision, and I would be pleased if you would keep your hands to yourself."

"Would you?"

She turned abruptly at the knowing look in his eye and started back to the village. He followed but did not attempt to accost her again. Still, she could feel his eyes on her back. She wasn't certain if her heart was pounding with such intensity because of that or because of her own rigid pace.

Wulfric left her at the edge of the village, and Arietta continued on alone until she reached the outskirts at the other end. She found Edwynn, his leather apron tied around him, working the bellows. Although it was early morning, he was already covered with ash and soot. He glanced up when she entered his shop.

"I will be with you soon. Have a seat."

Arietta seated herself on a stool, watching with interest as Edwynn continued to fire the furnace with the bellows. The temperatures were cold outside, but the shop was extremely warm, even with the large opening in the roof.

Sweat poured from Edwynn's face, and he brushed it aside with his shoulder.

"You wished to speak with me, Edwynn?"

He glanced at her briefly, his look resting briefly on her flushed cheeks and the wild disarray of her hair. Though the color in her cheeks could be attributed to the warm furnace, her mussed hair could not. When Edwynn's eyes met hers, Arietta's color deepened. She looked away, certain that he knew what had transpired between Wulfric and herself.

When Wulfric sauntered by the shop, he grinned at Arietta through the open door, giving Edwynn a brief, unsmiling nod.

"He wants you," Edwynn said unemotionally, watching Wulfric's retreating back.

Arietta gave a brittle laugh. "Do not be foolish."

Edwynn looked back at her, his eyes traveling over her in quiet inspection. He lifted his eyes to meet hers. "I am not being foolish. I have seen the way he looks at you. It is the same way Ingvar looks at my forged sword." He nodded to the gleaming instrument hanging over the door of the shop.

The bright alloy shone with pure intensity. Though the core was made of iron, it contained a rare steel edge. Edwynn had been offered a fortune for the piece, but he resisted all offers, saying that the sword was his perfect masterpiece.

Trying to lighten the mood, Arietta smiled. "Are you comparing me to a sword?"

Edwynn did not return her smile. "All women are like swords. They can cut the heart out of a man and leave him useless."

Arietta's eyes widened at this statement. "Edwynn," she asked hesitantly. "Have I done that to you?"

His surprised look turned to her. "I was not referring to anyone in particular," he denied softly. "It was just a thought."

Arietta somehow doubted it. There was something infinitely desperate in his low-toned voice.

"Wulfric cannot want me," she told him. "He has another woman. A Norsewoman. Her name is Wendella."

Edwynn turned back to the furnace, breaking open the bottom corner of the smelter. "Ah, the fair Wendella."

His sarcasm surprised Arietta. "You know her?"

He glanced at her briefly before turning back to his work, but in that split second, she knew. It was there in his eyes.

"I've done business with her," Edwynn answered carefully.

"You are in love with her," Arietta stated unequivocally.

His stunned eyes met hers, sudden color filling his face. "Now do not be foolish yourself."

Arietta sighed with resignation. She raised her face to the ceiling, closing her eyes, then stared hard at Edwynn. This is what she had been praying for, yet she was inexplicably hurt by the knowledge of his defection. "Edwynn, I release you from your vow to me."

He said nothing for a moment. He tapped off the slag from the smelter, revealing the ore bloom. Arietta could see that he was thinking hard about what to say.

"I have not asked to be released," he finally stated.

Arietta got up and went to him. She handed him his file

from the shelf, and he took it slowly, his eyes lifting in embarrassment to hers. "Nevertheless," she told him firmly. "I release you."

"And who will take care of you?"

Placing her hands on her hips, Arietta glared at him. "I have taken care of myself for some time now. I can continue to do so."

Edwynn snorted, moving his hands over the warm ore. He would not look at her. "Have you really taken care of yourself, Arietta?"

She opened her mouth to answer him in no uncertain terms, when suddenly she hesitated. Ever since her father had died, Edwynn had come to her to buy certain things. She made his bread, she wove his garments, and she sold him vegetables from her garden. There were others he could have purchased such goods from, but he had always come to her. Now she understood why. It was so that she would have an income for the things she couldn't do for herself. She looked at him, suddenly realizing all he had done for her.

"I can take care of myself," she repeated, suddenly uncertain that it was true. "You are free."

He dropped both ore and file to the ground, rising to stand beside her. His eyes were suddenly dark with fury. "Why, so that you can have Wulfric?"

"I never—"

"You can forget it. You may have released me, but I have not released you."

"But Edwynn—"

"This time next week," he said forcefully, "we will be wed."

Arietta's nostrils flared with anger. "I refuse."

"Do not make me take you before the folkmoot."

The color drained from Arietta's face. Never had she heard such a tone of voice from Edwynn. It frightened her almost as much as being threatened with the council. Her chest rose and fell rapidly in agitation. She stared at him, trying to find the jest in his words, but there was none. Turning, she left swiftly, knowing that he was still watching her.

Wulfric came to stand beside Edwynn, startling the other man with his sudden presence. Already angry, Edwynn's brow lowered further. "What do you want?" he snapped.

Wulfric's brooding gaze locked with Edwynn's wary one. Wulfric lifted his ax, stroking his thumb slowly along the edge.

"Gramr here needs a new edge," he answered softly.

Edwynn wavered, but finally motioned the Viking inside.

Wulfric lifted the ax to him with both hands, but when Edwynn reached to take it, the Viking's grip remained. Edwynn looked at the Norseman and almost recoiled from the darkness of his eyes.

They stood holding the ax together, both men aware that the other was a rival for both the woman, Arietta, and a place of honor in the village.

Wulfric slowly released the ax, watching as Edwynn turned to his whetstone. He did not trust the Englishman, and he stood tense, awaiting the man's next move.

It took Edwynn but a moment to bring a gleaming edge to the Norseman's ax with his grindstone. He hefted the tool, checking the edge with his own fingers. He looked at Wulfric and suddenly threw the ax to him. Wulfric deftly caught the instrument, his eyes never leaving Edwynn's.

"She is mine, Norseman," Edwynn said in an icy voice. "She will never have a pagan."

"There are some who have been added to your church by baptism that I would give the same name to," Wulfric told him, his voice dangerously low. "Many of my people have been forced to accept baptism and claim Christianity, yet in their hearts they are not. I see the same here."

"I do not know what you are talking about."

"Do you not?" Wulfric shifted the ax from his left hand to his right. "You may have her now, but can you *keep* her?"

Edwynn shrugged. "Arietta and I will be wed next week. I know that Viking women are allowed to divorce their husbands whenever they choose, but it is not *our* way. Besides,

Arietta would never do such a thing."

Wulfric dropped the ax to his side, his mouth tilted into a half-smile. "You do not really want to marry her, do you? There is another you wish to have instead."

Edwynn met Wulfric's knowing eye. The Englishman brushed a sooty hand through his already dark hair, unable to withstand the Norseman's gaze. Edwynn's body grew rigid with anger. "I have said that we will marry."

"And if there was an opportunity to do otherwise?"

Edwynn glanced at Wulfric suspiciously. "What are you suggesting?"

"In my country, when two men want the same woman, they go to a small island."

"And?"

Wulfric's eyes gleamed. "Only one returns."

Edwynn's eyes grew large. His gaze shifted to the ax clutched in the other man's hand, and he swallowed hard. "You are suggesting a fight?"

Wulfric merely lifted an eyebrow in challenge.

Edwynn picked up the ore and file he had dropped earlier. Taking the file, he swiped it across the surface of the ore. It tested with incredible hardness. He smiled slowly, looking at the Viking. "I have no need to fight when I have already won."

"I heard Arietta say that she released you," Wulfric countered harshly.

Edwynn stood uncowed. "Then you also heard me say that I refused to be released."

Wulfric folded his arms across his chest, his ax shining wickedly against his arm. "You would marry a woman who does not want you?"

"I promised her father that I would look after her."

Wulfric smiled slowly. "She will be looked after."

Edwynn's smile was just as slow. "You do not know Arietta like you think you do. I believe that, perhaps, you are in for a mighty surprise."

"You have been fair with your advice," Wulfric stated.

"Now let me give you some. *Never* let Wendella know that you are interested in her."

Edwynn did not answer, and Wulfric turned to leave. He glanced back over his shoulder. "I will never submit to Christianity for any woman," he declared.

Edwynn looked rather alarmed. "Then you will never have Arietta."

"We shall see."

seven

Friday dawned cold and wet. Arietta wrapped her cloak about her more thoroughly, blowing frost rings with her mouth as she hurried along to Gwyn's house.

Gwyn was home with only Helga to keep her company. She looked up when Arietta opened the door and peered inside. Gwyn's bright smile lightened her wan features. "Come in, Arietta. Come help Helga and me prepare the smoked fish for tonight's supper."

Arietta hurriedly closed the door behind her. The smoke from the fire pit lingered in the air, giving the atmosphere a thick, foglike appearance.

Arietta studied her sister's pale face. "Are you not well, Gwyn?"

Gwyn shrugged, one corner of her mouth tilting into a wry smile. "It is to be expected, I suppose."

It took Arietta a moment to understand, then she smiled brightly. "You are with child?"

At Gwyn's nod, Arietta let out a small whoop. "Gwyn, that is wonderful news. Does Sidroc know?"

Gwyn pulled the wooden cutting board forward on the small wooden table and began chopping the smoked fish. "I believe he suspects. I have not been well for the past several mornings."

Arietta hurried to her side, taking the knife from her fingers. "Here, let me do that. Why don't you sit down for awhile?"

"I have too much to do," Gwyn protested. "I need to card the wool, spin the flax, and set up my weaving frame."

Arietta flailed the knife at her sister. "That can wait for a time. I will help you with all of those things, but for now. . ." She smiled at Helga. "Why don't you take little Helga onto your lap and tell her a story?"

The little girl turned sparkling eyes to her mother. "Will you, Mutter?"

Gwyn looked from one to the other, her gaze resting longest on her child. "I suppose I have been neglecting you of late, is that not so my little Helga?" She turned relieved eyes to Arietta. "Thank you. I think I will do just that."

Arietta waited until the two were curled up together on one of the long benches framing the wall, then set to work preparing supper. She told Gwyn over her shoulder, "Speak up so that I can hear the story also."

All three were so engrossed in the story, they failed to hear the sounds from outside of the men returning until Bjorn came bursting through the door, his face ruddy with the cold. "Guess what we have done? We caught fifteen fish!"

Gwyn lifted an eyebrow. "Fifteen?" She looked past her son at Sidroc holding only four fish on a line. He flushed with color, using the excuse of giving the fish to Arietta to turn his eyes away.

Wulfric entered the house behind him, ducking his head to avoid hitting the low door beam. "My fault, Gwyn. I gave some of them away."

Gwyn's eyes grew tender as she stared at each one of her men. "I understand," she answered softly.

Sidroc crossed to her side, kneeling before her. His brow puckered into a frown.

"Are you not feeling well?"

She lifted a hand, stroking his cheek. "I am fine. Arietta thought I might like to tell little Helga a story."

Helga distracted the family patriarch by bursting into speech about the story she had just been told. "And Aunt Arietta says that the story is true! God came and lived on earth like a man!"

Wulfric stood behind Arietta, peering over her shoulder. He sighed, his lips tilting wryly, and Arietta felt her heart give a quick little hop. Her fingers became suddenly clumsy.

"And does it say somewhere in your holy words that a man must eat fish every Friday?"

Arietta refused to look into his eyes, knowing how much they affected her.

"It is in commemoration of the day the Lord died on the cross," she told him softly.

"But does it say in your holy words that you must?" he persisted.

Arietta was silent a long time. When she glanced up, she found Gwyn and Sidroc curiously awaiting her answer, their eyes intent.

"I have not found it so," she finally answered.

Wulfric shook his head. "Better to worship Thor. At least *he* understands a man's desires."

Arietta threw him a scathing look, angered by his suggestion. She noticed the twinkle in his eye and realized that he was trying to rile her. Ignoring him, she smiled at Bjorn. "And how many fish did *you* catch, Bjorn?"

Bjorn's puffed out chest suddenly deflated. He shifted his feet awkwardly, peeking at Arietta from under lowered lids. "None."

"He was too concerned with playing in the forest," his father told them, his voice slightly harsh. "It is time that he begin to act like a man."

"It will be two years before he is legally so," Arietta interrupted in irritation. "He is still a child."

Five pair of eyes fastened themselves on her, and Arietta stopped, horrified that she had intervened between father and son. She placed her hand over her mouth, her contrite eyes meeting Sidroc's. "I beg pardon," she whispered.

Sidroc's eyes were carefully blank. Not so Wulfric's. His gleamed with suppressed anger.

Bjorn stared at her, his look one of extreme disgust. "I am *not* a child!"

Disconcerted, Arietta looked from Gwyn to Sidroc. "Truly, I apologize." She wiped her hands carefully on a cloth and retrieved her cloak. "I must go and attend to things at home."

"You need not leave," Sidroc answered her softly. "Gwyn was expecting you to share the meal with us."

Anxious to get away, Arietta gave him a half-hearted smile. "Another time."

Gwyn met her at the door, her eyes pleading. "Please stay."

Arietta placed a comforting hand on her arm. "Another time, Gwyn. I really need to go."

She saw Wulfric coming toward her, so she ducked out the door, hurrying down the path that led to the village. She might have saved herself the trouble. He easily caught up with her, matching his steps to hers.

"Norse children are taught differently than English. It is necessary."

"Why?" Arietta spat back. "So that they can learn to *viking,* killing and plundering?"

He pulled her to a stop, his blue eyes stormy and dark. "No," he disagreed. "So that they can survive the harsh land they live in. Too many of our children die young as it is."

Arietta remembered Gwyn saying that she had already lost a child. She did not know what to say. She pulled away from his hand and continued on her way. Wulfric caught up with her again.

"I wondered if you might do me a favor," he asked hesitantly, and Arietta thought the words had probably choked him.

"I might," she answered back but continued walking. She heard him sigh and stifled a grin.

"The woman Martha is ill."

Arietta whirled to face him in concern. The move caught him unawares, and he collided into her and would have sent her crashing to the ground if not for his quick reflexes. His fingers had closed around her forearms but then slid down to capture her hands. She tried to pull away, but he lifted one of her hands to mold it against his larger one, and she suddenly forgot what she had been about to say.

Wulfric stared at their two hands for a long time. When he

looked into her eyes, she felt her heart begin to thump errati-
cally. There was something in his eyes she had never seen
before, and it frightened her.

"You are so tiny," he told her throatily. "I could crush you
with my bare hands."

"I am not so easily broken, Wulfric."

He did not answer her, and she pulled her hand away. "Tell
me about Martha."

He crossed his arms over his chest, the long-sleeved shirt
straining against his muscles. His eyes narrowed. "She is ill,
I do not know with what. When I passed by earlier there was
no fire going, so I checked on her. I am afraid that I frighten
the children."

Arietta fought the smile that threatened. "Surely not."

The look he gave her spoke volumes. "Will you come
with me?"

Arietta did not hesitate. "Of course. Is she one of those
you gave fish to?"

He jerked his head in a nod, watching as she stuck a forefinger in her mouth, her forehead puckered in concentration.
"If she has no fire, then I should get some from Gwyn."

"That is not necessary. I have a steel and some flint."

Relieved, Arietta smiled. "Good. That will save time." She
turned off the path and began making her way toward
Martha's house.

"How is Wiglaf?" she threw over her shoulder.

"He beat me at *hnefatafl*."

Arietta almost stopped walking again. She glanced at
Wulfric with a grin.

He lifted his brow, his mouth quirking. "The idea appeals
to you, does it not?"

She kept walking, trying to keep the smile from her face. It
would never do for Wulfric to know that she and Wiglaf had
been playing the game as well and that she had beaten
Wiglaf only last week.

When they emerged from the woods, Arietta shivered at the

coldness of the hut before her. No welcoming smoke came from the hole in the roof, no children played in the yard as was usual, no light emanated from the darkened shutters.

Arietta tapped on the door, waiting until Judith slowly creaked it open a crack. Her eyes went past Arietta, growing large when she saw the Norseman.

"It is all right, Judith. Wulfric and I are here to help."

Reluctantly, the little girl opened the door wider. Though Wulfric smiled, Judith never responded.

Arietta went past her and hurried to Martha's bed. Asimund lay next to her, quietly stroking his mother's forehead. He held a finger to his lips to silence them. "She is asleep."

Arietta reached out, laying a hand upon Martha's forehead. It was hot to the touch. She turned to tell Wulfric but found him gone. She smiled reassuringly at Asimund. "I will be right back."

She went to the door and found Wulfric outside using his ax to deftly split some wood into kindling. He glanced up.

"I need some water," Arietta told him. "Could you bring me some?"

"Let me get the fire going first, then I will get you some water."

She nodded and turned back to the room. The place looked as though a good storm had blown through. Before she could do anything about that, she must first see to Judith, Bertin, and Asimund.

Kneeling before Judith, she asked the little girl, "Are you hungry?"

Judith nodded her head slightly, her thumb stuck firmly in her mouth. Her large eyes were glassy, and Arietta wasn't certain if she was getting sick or was simply hungry. Bertin sat huddled against the wall, his little body shivering against the cold.

Taking off her cloak, Arietta wrapped it firmly around Judith and told her to go lie down with her brother on the bed. She picked up Bertin and settled him in beside the others. The room was as cold as ice, and she feared for them all.

Wulfric came into the hut and started a fire with his flint and steel, under the watchful eyes of the children. Arietta wondered what would have happened to the three if not for Wulfric. She took one of the fish Wulfric had left earlier and began preparing it.

When the fire was burning well, Wulfric came to her side. "What else can I do?"

"The water?" she reminded him, and he nodded, quickly exiting the hut.

Arietta took a small frying pan from the wall, setting it over the fire. After cleaning the bones from the fish, she dropped it into the sizzling skillet. Before long, the mouth-watering scent of frying fish filled the hut.

The children watched appreciatively, swallowing as their mouths filled with saliva. Arietta smiled.

"It is almost ready."

She left the fish frying and returned to check on Martha. It concerned her that the woman hadn't awakened even with all the noise and movement.

Wulfric brought her the water. Judith shied away from his tall frame, but Asimund, growing more bold, stared at the Viking. "You are the one who brings us food," he stated with certainty.

Wulfric merely lifted an eyebrow in that typical way of his.

As the fire burned, some of the chill left the hut, but it remained frightfully cold. Arietta shivered, wishing that she had thought to bring along an extra cloak. Wulfric looked at her questioningly, then glanced around the room until his eyes focused on Judith, whose large brown eyes peeped out at him from beneath the confines of Arietta's cloak.

He turned to Arietta in exasperation. "I will go and see if Gwyn can spare a blanket."

"Thank you."

He grunted and disappeared out the door.

Arietta took the cold water and a rag and began washing

Martha's face. The woman opened fever-dulled eyes, her face filled with confusion.

"It is all right, Martha," Arietta soothed. "You are sick, and we are here to help."

Martha gave a feeble nod, then closed her eyes once more in sleep. Relief and thankfulness had flashed from her eyes for a brief instant.

Arietta had the children fed and settled around their mother when Wulfric returned. He brought with him a basket of food and several wolf pelt blankets. "Gwyn says to let her know if there is anything else she can do."

Arietta took the basket of food, setting it on the table. "Tell her thank you for me."

"Are you staying here the night?"

Arietta looked at him in surprise. "Of course. Martha is too ill to take care of herself, and the children are too young."

"Then I am staying also."

Arietta would have argued, but the set of Wulfric's broad shoulders told her not to bother. He prepared a pallet where he could rest, then made one for Arietta closer to the fire.

Arietta cleaned the second fish that Wulfric had left so that she could feed him some supper. After cooking it, she added bread from Gwyn's basket to his plate, and handing him a spoon and knife, she watched while he settled himself to eat.

His look fastened on her. "Are you not eating?"

She shrugged, knowing that food would not settle on her nervous stomach. "I am not hungry yet. Maybe later."

He quirked a brow at her but did not pursue the issue. After he finished eating, he went back outside to cut more wood for the fire.

Arietta had used some of the fish to make a broth, hoping that she could get Martha to eat a little. When the children were asleep, she roused Martha and tried to spoon some of the broth into the woman's weak mouth. She managed to get at least half a bowl down her before Martha closed her eyes in sleep again.

Arietta set the house to rights, noticing that Martha had no oil for the lamp. It would soon be dark, then they would have no light. She told Wulfric when he returned to the hut. He glanced at the clay lamp, then back at her. "There is none?"

Arietta shook her head, and Wulfric sighed heavily. "I will return shortly."

It was some time before she saw the bobbing light of a torch coming through the forest. Already darkness had descended, and Arietta stood at the open window, ignoring the cold that seeped in. Seeing Wulfric, she let out her breath in relief.

He came into the house, dumping a bag on the table. Arietta used his torchlight to identify the items she needed, adding fish oil to the clay pot, then a moss wick. Wulfric lit the lamp with his torch and snuffed the torch out on the ground outside.

"What else can I do?" he asked.

Arietta's eyes met his, and though she knew he would never admit it, she could see the tiredness there. "There is nothing more that you can do. Get some sleep."

He checked the hut before settling down before the door. Before long, Arietta heard the soft timber of his even breathing.

She finished what she was doing, then checked on Martha. The fever seemed to be receding, and Arietta breathed a silent prayer of relief. Pulling her wolf pelts close to the bed, she settled down close to Martha's side. She wrapped one pelt around her, snuggling into its warmth.

Though she was tired, she couldn't sleep. In only four days, she would become Edwynn's wife. The thought curled her stomach. She looked across at Wulfric's sleeping form and knew the reason why.

How had it happened? How could she possibly love a heathen? It went against everything she believed in. Her lips curled into a soft smile. Heathen he might be, but despite his rough and tough exterior, he had a kind and generous heart. Edwynn, though a Christian, often decried her spending her time helping others, but Wulfric did it without thought to himself. The Scriptures taught that to do so was the same as doing it for Christ. To deny help to others was to deny it to the Lord.

Edwynn claimed to be a Christian, but was he truly one in heart? The church taught that anyone living in England must be baptized in the name of Christ, yet murders, thefts, and other atrocities abounded.

What the people did not seem to understand was that merely being baptized and claiming Christianity did not make you a Christian. Jesus had said that you must love the Lord with all your heart, soul, and mind and love your neighbor as yourself.

Wulfric certainly seemed to embody the message, yet he refused to bow to Christ. She frowned heavily. What then made the difference in him? Did Thor teach such philosophies? Somehow, she doubted it. She had heard about Vikings slaying innocent people to offer to their gods.

Then what could account for Wulfric's behavior? Had Gwyn somehow been able to influence him, or was he, as the Scriptures stated in Paul's letter to the Romans, doing by nature the things required by the law? That thought gave her hope that he might some day bow his knee to the Lord Jesus Christ and become a true Christian.

But to what end? She bit her lip, realizing the futility of this thinking. In four short days, she would belong to another man, and she must purge thoughts of Wulfric from her mind. She lifted a prayer heavenward, asking for God's intercession in the matter, but knowing she would do His will, come what may.

Dawn approached with rapid wings, and still Arietta sat staring at the man she had grown to love. Her eyes were gritty from lack of sleep, but her mind simply would not shut down. For some reason she felt the need to watch Wulfric as much as possible, to imprint his image into her mind.

He suddenly rolled over, capturing her gaze, and Arietta realized that he had been awake for some time. There was a yearning in his eyes she had never seen before.

They broke eye contact only when Martha's voice inter-rupted them. "Arietta?"

Arietta sprang to her feet. She felt the other woman's fore-head, her face creasing into a smile. "The fever is gone."

Martha stretched as much as the three little bodies snug-gled next to her would allow. A slow smile spread across her face. "I feel much better today."

The three children started stirring. Arietta helped Judith and Bertin from the bed, watching with a smile as they stum-bled across the floor, their tousled heads disappearing out the door. Within moments, they had returned shivering, wide-eyed, and ready for the day's adventures.

Wulfric replenished the fire, then gave Asimund a flint and steel. He showed him how to work the combination to start a fire. "The next time the fire goes out, you must start it again."

Asimund's eyes shone with gratitude at the responsibility. His small chest puffed out with pride, and for the first time, Arietta realized just how much acting like a man meant to a young boy. Wulfric's "I told you so" look only irritated her.

After seeing that everyone was fed, Arietta left with the promise to return later in the day. She walked along the path, Wulfric behind her. It seemed the tiredness that she had held at bay was coming upon her in a rush. She stumbled and would have fallen, but Wulfric caught her up in his arms. He stared down into her exhausted face, frowning.

"I am all right," Arietta rebuked him. "Put me down."

Wulfric ignored the command. "Close your eyes, Arietta, and sleep."

She thought of fighting him, but her body would not respond to any of her commands. Of their own volition, her eyes fluttered, then closed altogether. She dropped her head to Wulfric's chest, and within seconds, she was fast asleep.

Wulfric stood transfixed by the sleeping woman in his arms. She brought out every protective instinct that he'd tried to keep buried deep inside of him. Never had a woman so touched his mind, and yes, even his heart.

He wanted Arietta more than he had ever wanted anything in his life. It was a battle to keep his Norse blood from making him do something they would both regret. That she was not beautiful mattered not one whit to him. Beauty though she was, Wendella had never been able to worm her way into his mind the way this woman had.

He shifted her in his arms, then continued on his way, his mind still full of conflict.

When he reached the clearing in front of Sidroc's hut, he found Sidroc coming toward him. "I was just coming to find you."

He looked at Arietta in Wulfric's arms, his eyes lifting to Wulfric's in question.

"I think she must not have slept all night."

Sidroc looked back at Arietta. "Bring her inside. We will wait until she has some rest before giving her the bad news."

Wulfric halted. "What bad news?"

"Edwynn, the smith, has been seriously hurt."

eight

Several hours later Arietta awakened to the sound of scraping. She slowly opened her eyes and saw Gwyn sitting across the room, carding her wool.

Arietta lifted herself to a sitting position, throwing her legs over the side of the wooden bunk. She placed one hand to her swimming head, trying to still its rhythmic movement.

Gwyn placed the two spiked brushes on the table and came to sit beside Arietta. No one else was in the hut.

"Where is everyone?"

"Wulfric and Sidroc took the children with them. They said you needed the rest."

Arietta's mind was beginning to clear. "How did I get here?"

"Wulfric carried you," Gwyn explained. "You have slept a long time. How are you feeling?"

"Hungry."

Gwyn laughed, rising to her feet. "I will get you something to eat." She placed slices of cheese on bread and handed it Arietta, who wolfed the lot down, drinking the cup of goat's milk that Gwyn placed next to her.

"Arietta, there's something I have to tell you."

Arietta licked her fingers clean of the cheese residue.

"Edwynn has been injured," her sister continued.

Dropping her hand slowly to her lap, Arietta grew very still. "How?"

Gwyn sighed, getting up and crossing to pick up her carding implements. She began scraping the brushes together without looking at Arietta. Knowing her sister, Arietta realized that something was bothering Gwyn that she was reluctant to divulge. "Tell me. How serious is it?"

Gwyn lifted her head and stared ahead unseeing. She glanced at Arietta, then continued with what she was doing. Finally she spoke. "Someone tried to kill Godfred. Edwynn stopped them."

The blood drained from Arietta's face, her body going cold all over. "I cannot believe it."

"Well, it is true. A man from the village was about to shoot an arrow at Godfred when Edwynn noticed him and shoved Godfred aside. The arrow pierced Edwynn's chest instead."

Arietta came to her feet. "I have to go to him."

Gwyn placed her carding tools back on the table. "Of course, but please wait for Wulfric to walk you to the village."

Arietta was already heading for the door. "I cannot. I have to see how badly Edwynn is hurt."

Though she might not love Edwynn as she loved Wulfric, she loved him nonetheless. He had always been good to her and her father, and although he aggravated her at times, he was her very good friend.

"Arietta!" Gwyn called.

Arietta turned sharply. "Do they know who did this?"

Gwyn was distressed, that much was obvious. "It was Aelwyn." She placed a detaining hand on Arietta's arm. "Please wait for Wulfric."

"I will be fine." She hugged Gwyn, then pushed her gently away. "I am not certain when I will be able to return." She grabbed her cloak from the peg by the door and quickly hastened out into the cold before Gwyn could stop her, heading swiftly for the village.

When she reached Edwynn's hut, she found several people gathered around it, murmuring amongst themselves. She pushed her way through, knocking briefly on the door and entering at Edwynn's quiet voice bidding her come.

The room was semidark from a dwindling fire, the shutters of the windows closed against the biting cold. Godfred sat on the stool next to the bed, Wendella standing at his side. Both turned at her entrance. Though Godfred's eyes were wary,

Wendella's shot sparks of pure rage.

Arietta nodded briefly to the two, then quietly took Edwynn's good hand, kneeling beside the straw bed. His face was beaded with sweat even though the room was fairly cold. She had never seen him so lacking in color. A bandage was wound round his bare chest, binding his arm against his side.

"How are you?" she asked quietly, her searching gaze moving quickly over him.

"I am beginning to believe that I will live," he croaked, his lips tilted with humor.

Wendella stepped forward, her eyes softening when they rested on Edwynn. "He saved my brother's life, and I will be eternally grateful."

Godfred smiled fondly at his sister, taking her by the hand. He looked at Arietta, the wariness still in his eyes.

"The man who did this has eluded us, although we know who it was. The village has called for the folkmoot as soon as the ealdorman returns."

Arietta's glance went from one to the other. "Were there other witnesses?"

"Several," Wendella bit out harshly. She threw her long braids over her shoulder, her stance rigid. She reminded Arietta of a female version of Wulfric. The comparison unsettled her.

"It was Aelwyn," Edwynn whispered.

"I know," she said. "Gwyn told me."

His eyes met Arietta's, and a look of understanding passed between them. Aelwyn was the same age as Arietta, and they were close friends. Everyone in the village loved him, for he was kind and generous to a fault. That he could do such a thing was incredible to everyone.

"Why would he do such a thing?" Wendella choked out. She glared at Arietta as though it were all her fault. "What has my brother ever done to him? Your people call us heathens and savages, but what are they? They should all be slain!"

Arietta answered her softly, trying to stem the tide of rising fury. "Ten years ago when your people came to our village, they murdered Aelwyn's mother."

Godfred jerked his head up sharply but said nothing. Wendella was not so reticent. "My brother had nothing to do with that. He was not on that raid."

"But Aelwyn blames all Norsemen, just as you are blaming all the English for this deed."

Wendella stared at Arietta a long time. Several times she opened her mouth to speak, but no words came. She finally retreated into silence.

Edwynn tugged on Arietta's hand, and she turned her attention back to him. At his uneasy look, Arietta tensed.

"I am sorry, Arietta, but I think we must postpone the wedding."

Arietta's heart gave a quick leap. She had forgotten the forthcoming wedding in all the excitement. But the relief that flooded through her also brought a deep sense of guilt.

"That is all right, Edwynn. There will be another time."

Wendella's eyes narrowed, and she silently studied the two. She turned back to her brother. "We must go."

He nodded and rose to his feet. "I owe you my life, Edwynn. Whatever you need, you have only to ask."

Edwynn's eyes flicked briefly to Wendella, but the girl had already turned away, missing the look. Arietta, however, did not, nor did Godfred. He cast an anxious glance at Arietta, opening his mouth to say something. When Wendella turned back to Edwynn with a smile, Godfred pressed his lips together tightly.

"I will come again tomorrow to check on you," Wendella announced. "As my brother says, whatever we have is yours."

A closed look shuttered Edwynn's face. He took Arietta's hand and began stroking it. "There is no need, Wendella. Arietta will care for my needs."

Wendella's vivid blue eyes darkened with anger. Pressing her lips together, she turned and shoved her way out the door. Godfred stared after her, his look one of utter confusion.

Shrugging, he gave Edwynn a lopsided smile. "I leave you in good hands. I will see you on the morrow."

Edwynn nodded, and the Norseman left.

Edwynn turned his head so he could more comfortably see Arietta. "You look tired. What have you been doing?"

"Not very much," she said, not wanting to bring up the subject of helping Martha when she knew how he opposed such action. "I was at Gwyn's when they told me of your accident."

One corner of his forehead lifted slightly. "Accident?"

She sat down on the stool Godfred had vacated, fixing her long woolen skirt until it warmed her chilled legs. "You know what I mean." Arietta stared off into space for some time, not realizing that Edwynn was watching her. "What do you think will happen with Aelwyn?"

"I am not certain," Edwynn answered softly. "The folk-moot will have to decide."

"He could lose his land."

"Arietta."

Recognizing the urgency in his voice, Arietta tilted her head at him. "Yes?"

"I wish to release you from your promise to marry me."

Surprised, Arietta stared back at him. "Why?"

Edwynn tilted his head back on the pillow until he was staring at the ceiling. His jaw clenched and unclenched several times before he finally spoke. "I did not want to say anything in front of the others, but the muscles in my arm have been injured pretty badly. I probably will not be able to work a forge again."

Arietta frowned. "But what has that to do with our marriage?"

Edwynn took a deep breath, glaring at her. "Do you not understand. I can no longer support you."

It took her a moment to follow his reasoning, then her green eyes grew stormy. "And you think that I would leave you because of that?"

His jaw worked convulsively, his nostrils flaring in anger. "I will be a beggar! Do you not understand that?"

Arietta got quickly to her feet, too perturbed to stay in one place. She paced the small confines of Edwynn's hut, twining her hands in agitation. "How little you must think of me," she whispered harshly, and his eyes widened in surprise at her tone.

She came back to the bed, leaning over him. "Now you listen to me, Edwynn. Our marriage may have been postponed, but a promise is a promise. Would you go back on your word?"

"I will not have you married to a cripple!" he shouted angrily.

"Do not make me take you before the folkmoot," she told him quietly, repeating his earlier words.

"Arietta."

She placed a finger over his lips, smiling slightly. "Enough for now. Just get well."

His eyes softened. "I really do love you, you know."

She gave him a half-grin. "I know, but not like you love Wendella. If only there was some way for the two of you—"

"There is not," he interrupted ruthlessly. "A Viking woman would never accept a weak man, and you know it."

Arietta shrugged, unaccountably hurt that he hadn't bothered to deny it. "Then I guess you are stuck with me."

"Arietta!"

"Go to sleep. You need your rest. I will return to check on you later. Is there anything that you need?"

He shook his head slightly. Bending over, she brushed her lips across his cheek. Wrinkling her nose, she rubbed her fingers lightly over his jaw. "A shave perhaps?"

He grinned. "I apologize. I have not had the time." He glanced down at his arm. "Nor the energy."

Laughing, Arietta went to the door, commanding over her shoulder, "Go to sleep."

She was met outside the door by several concerned faces.

"He is well for now," she told them. She looked at one young man hovering on the edge of the group. "Bass, will you please keep Edwynn's fire going?"

The boy stepped forward. "Yes, Arietta, I will do that."

She smiled her thanks, turning to find Wulfric stalking toward her, his face as black as a thundercloud. The others departed hastily to their homes when the Norseman strode into their midst. "You should have waited," he ground out savagely.

Arietta's eyebrows lifted. "I have walked this village for all of my life. I am in no danger here."

Wulfric's jaw tightened, a tick forming in his cheek. "There is a madman on the loose," he retorted through gritted teeth.

Recognizing his concern, Arietta nevertheless had to make him understand. "Aelwyn is no madman. He is full of hatred and anger, but he is not insane."

"Hatred and anger breed insanity," he returned, his voice tight with suppressed feelings.

Arietta's face softened. "Maybe so, but Aelwyn would never hurt me."

When she went to walk by him, he grabbed her forearm, his eyes meeting hers. It seemed an eternity before Arietta pulled her arm from his grasp. She walked ahead of him, aware of his seething look scorching her back.

When she would have turned into her own gate, Wulfric stopped her. "Gwyn is expecting you."

Arietta sighed, rubbing her neck tiredly. She rolled her head on her shoulders. "Tell her that I will come tomorrow."

"And Martha?"

She closed her small gate between them. "I told her that I would return today, and I will."

"You are going to wear yourself out."

The smile she gave him reached all the way to her eyes. "I am not too tired to play you a game of *hnefatafl*."

He met the dare head on. "When?"

"Since I promised Gwyn that I would help with her spinning and weaving, tell her that I will come tomorrow. After that, I will play you a game."

"I will look forward to it," he told her, his eyes sparkling.

Arietta watched him walk away, wondering what form of

insanity had come over her. All Wulfric needed was another challenge, but then maybe playing the game would take his mind off other pursuits.

She went inside her hut, closing the door against the cold winter air. Taking the flint and steel, she started a fire in her fire pit. The room was freezing. She climbed the ladder to her room, grabbing a blanket off the bed and dragging it with her back to the main room.

Wrapping the blanket around her, she huddled near the fire, her mind already wandering in different directions. That she wanted to spend time with Wulfric was beyond her denial, but she knew it would not be wise. The more time she spent in his presence, the harder it became to keep her feelings hidden.

Then there was poor Edwynn. Her heart swelled with pride in him that he had risked his own life to save that of a despised Norseman. Had Godfred been able to overcome Edwynn's fear and animosity merely by doing business with him? They had seemed on rather friendly terms.

And what now? If Edwynn couldn't work his tools, what would he do for a living? The more she thought about it, the more she concluded that there was really no option. She couldn't turn her back on Edwynn now.

He was right. A Viking woman would hate weakness in a man. It was too bad that Wendella would not be able to see past Edwynn's affliction to the kind man within.

As the fire warmed the room, Arietta's thoughts grew hazy, her head bobbing with drowsiness. Before long, she was fast asleep.

❧

Wulfric watched Arietta's cottage until he saw her come out the door. He waited until she was some distance into the forest before he joined her. She glanced at him in surprise. "Where did you come from?"

He ignored the question, asking one of his own. "You are going to Martha's?"

"I am."

He reached to take the basket from her arms so that she would be free to shield herself from the wind with her woolen cloak. She thanked him politely, wrapping the cloak tightly around her.

Arietta looked at Wulfric askance. "Do you not ever feel the cold?"

He wore a fur vest and long sleeves, but still he seemed impervious to the freezing temperatures. He laughed lightly. "You think this is cold?"

Arietta's look went over him from head to toe. She envied him in his *puttee* leg bindings, and trousers. Even under her *cyrtel* and tunic she was freezing. "I suppose it gets much colder in Norway."

A twinkle lit his eyes. "Indeed it does."

They continued the rest of the way in companionable silence and found Martha on her feet. She was weak, but she promised to pace herself and let them know if she needed anything. Then she took Wulfric's large hand into hers, bending her head to press her lips against it. When she straightened, Martha smiled into the Norseman's eyes. "Thank you. Thank you for everything."

Arietta hid a laugh behind a cough as embarrassed color swept through Wulfric's face. He glared at Arietta, defying her to say anything. She prudently remained silent.

Martha thanked Arietta as well, but she gave Arietta a hug.

When they left, Wulfric walked beside Arietta this time, his frown thoughtful.

"What are you thinking?" she asked him softly.

He hesitated slightly. "Tell me about your God," he requested quietly.

Surprised, Arietta felt a small glow that grew into a burning flame. She told him of the Scriptures and things the church had always taught. She explained her thoughts and feelings about the verses Brother Bertrand had taught her and the other young people as they copied the texts for him.

Wulfric listened to her intently. When she spoke of God, she forgot who she was talking to. She opened herself to Wulfric like a flower to the sun. Suddenly, she stopped where the two paths diverged, one to the village, the other to Gwyn's. "I must return to the village," she said. "I need to check on Edwynn."

Wulfric's eyes darkened. "Edwynn was a very brave man to do what he did. Not many people would take an arrow meant for another."

Arietta met his eyes. "Edwynn is a Christian," she said simply.

"And that makes a difference? What has your God really done for you?" Wulfric asked, not certain he wanted to know.

"He promises us eternal life with Him. A life of beauty and peace. A place where there are no tears, no fighting, no hatred." She tilted her head. "What do your gods offer you?"

Wulfric remained silent.

Shrugging her shoulders slightly, Arietta said, "Tell Gwyn that I will come early tomorrow."

Wulfric glanced down at her. "I will tell her when I see her. Right now I am walking you to Edwynn's."

"Wulfric." Arietta sighed with annoyance but did not argue further. She allowed him to walk with her until she reached Edwynn's house. Aggravated with his insistence on following her around, she did not bother to thank him for his undesired protection. She knocked on the door briefly, entering quickly and shutting Wulfric out.

Edwynn turned his head toward her when she entered. The flames in his fire pit were burning brightly, taking much of the chill from the room. After the cool, clear air outside, Arietta squinted her eyes against the smoke in the room.

"Are you feeling better?" she asked him, crossing the room and laying a hand against his forehead.

He took the hand and pushed it away irritably. "I am well."

There was a knock at the door, and Arietta went to answer it, confused by Edwynn's surliness. An old woman from the village stood outside, a pot in her hands. "I have brought some soup for Edwynn."

Arietta smiled, opening the door wider. "Bring it in, Werburg."

The old woman wrinkled her nose, handing the pot to Arietta. "No, that is all right. You can give it to him."

Arietta reached for the pot, her look tender when she smiled at the other woman. "Are you certain?" At the other woman's vehement nod of the head, Arietta shifted the pot into her own arms. "Thank you, Werburg."

She watched the other woman scurry away before turning back to the room. Edwynn lay with his face away from her, his body tense. Frowning, Arietta set the pot on the table. "What is it, Edwynn? Are you hurting?"

When he turned his head back to her, tears hovered on the fringes of his eyes. "Arietta, I have been so wrong."

Seeing the tears, Arietta became alarmed. It was so unusual for her unemotional Edwynn to display any kind of feelings. "What have you been wrong about, Edwynn?"

She sat down on the stool, taking his hand into hers. He squeezed her fingers lightly.

"I have always complained about the way you help others, but now I see that it is the way you show love and concern. All day, people have been bringing me things or stopping by to see if I need anything. Even people I complained about when you were helping them." He sighed heavily. "Many have taken the little they have and have given it to me."

Glad that Edwynn had finally seen the light, Arietta twined her fingers with his. He looked into her eyes, and she smiled. "You have done a lot for these people, Edwynn. They appreciate you."

He snorted. "What have I ever done for them that it did not cost them?"

"You came and lived here when you could have made a fortune had you lived in another town. They appreciate that."

His look brightened. "You mean that?"

"Of course I do," she chided. "When have you ever known me to say something that I did not mean?"

He looked relieved and happier than Arietta had seen him for some time. "Thank you, Arietta."

She smiled, getting to her feet. "Well, I can see that I am not needed here. I will leave you in other capable hands."

By the time she left Edwynn's house, the winter sun was waning. It would soon be dark, and for the first time that Arietta could remember, she loathed the idea of returning to her lonely house. Then she noticed Wulfric leaning back against Edwynn's house, his arms crossed, one foot resting on the house behind him. He stood away from the wall when he saw her, glanced over her head to the door beyond, then returned his gaze to her face. "Well? How is he?"

Arietta smiled, suddenly glad to have Wulfric waiting for her. "He is well. There is no fever, and the villagers are caring for him. He has discovered that he is greatly loved."

Wulfric's look was intense. "And you? Have you discovered that you love him too?"

The smile fled from Arietta's face. She moved past Wulfric, walking toward her own house. "I have always loved Edwynn," she told him firmly.

He took her by the arm, turning her to face him. "I do not believe you."

She placed her hands on her hips and glared at him. "You do not *want* to believe me."

She managed to make it to her own yard before he jerked her to a stop. His eyes glittered dangerously. Pulling her into his arms, he kissed her with an intensity that left her breathless.

Setting her away from him, he slowly shook his head, backing toward the gate. "No, I do not want to believe you."

nine

Gwyn wound a batch of wool around a short wooden stick. She studied her sister carefully, frowning when Arietta jumped once again as the door was slung open and Helga raced inside.

Grabbing her carved wooden horse, the little girl once more raced back outside, slamming the door behind her.

"You certainly are jumpy today," Gwyn quietly observed.

Arietta glanced at her briefly, her face coloring hotly. She took the rod Gwyn handed her and carefully twisted a small portion of yarn into a thread, attaching it to the distaff wheel. She stood, ignoring her sister's probing look.

"Are not Sidroc and Wulfric looking for a place to grow crops?" she asked Gwyn.

Gwyn's look told Arietta that her sister knew she was avoiding the subject. Shrugging off the unspoken message, Arietta positioned herself with the pole cradled against her shoulder and the distaff wheel hanging down.

Gwyn set the distaff spinning. She sat back, picking up her carding brushes, and answered Arietta's earlier question. "The men are looking for crop land. Though the Norse have a reputation as bloodthirsty killers, most live like everyone else. They grow crops and animals, and they live a relatively normal life." Gwyn's look became grave with hidden remembrances. "But the good Lord help everyone when boredom sets in."

While Arietta continued to spin, Gwyn took her brushes and began to card more wool. She smiled at Arietta. "I really appreciate your help. Sometimes, spinning is a tedious job."

Arietta returned her smile. "I have found that it is when I do my best thinking."

"What do you think about?"

Just then the distaff wheel touched the floor. Gwyn set aside her carding tools and wound the lengthened thread around the distaff and set it spinning again. Arietta thanked her, then continued letting out small tufts of the wool. "Lately," Arietta said, "I have been thinking much about the Scriptures."

Gwyn looked up at her, her expression solemn. "I wish that I knew them as you do."

"I can teach you." Arietta's eyes lit up with the idea. "I could teach Bjorn and Helga as well."

Gwyn wound the thread as Arietta continued to spin. The carding tools lay forgotten in her lap, and Gwyn's sparkling green eyes met her sister's with resolve. "I would love that."

Arietta nodded with pleasure. "Then we will do so."

They worked throughout the morning until it was time to prepare the first meal of the day. Arietta continued spinning, while Gwyn prepared food for her family.

"Arietta."

Something in her sister's voice alerted Arietta, and she paused in her work. "Yes?"

"I understand that Edwynn has postponed your wedding."

Arietta used the pretext of winding the spun wool to look away from her sister's worried look. "That is so."

Gwyn set down her knife and crossed to Arietta's side. "Winter is setting in with a vengeance. What will you do? Edwynn can no longer care for you."

Arietta shrugged her shoulders, still not looking at her sister. "Then I will care for him."

"Sidroc says that the animal's skins are much fuller this year. He says that it will be a long, hard winter."

Finally meeting Gwyn's eyes, Arietta frowned. "Gwyn," she remonstrated. "I will get by. I always have."

Gwyn's look was full of frustration. "But always before you had Edwynn to help you. It will be some time before Edwynn is healed well enough to do anything, and even then, his arm will be useless."

"What do you suggest, Gwyn? That I leave Edwynn to fend for himself after he has cared for me for so many years?"

Sighing, Gwyn pressed her lips tightly together. "No, but you could move in with us. Sidroc would be glad to have you. He has already told me so."

Tingles shot through Arietta's body at the suggestion. Her breathing quickened, the mere thought of being in such close proximity to Wulfric threatening her poise. "I cannot."

"Because of Wulfric?"

Gwyn's knowing look did nothing for Arietta's composure. Of late, Wulfric had taken a much too personal interest in her welfare. It hadn't surprised her that he had been waiting this morning to escort her to Gwyn's house. He still considered Aelwyn a threat. The thing that bothered Arietta the most was not knowing what it was that Wulfric wanted from her.

"I cannot because I need to be close to Edwynn."

Gwyn shook her head in disbelief. "That is not why at all."

The opening of the door effectively ended their conversation. Sidroc entered, followed by a laughing Wulfric and the two giggling children.

Sidroc glanced from the tense expression of his wife, to the even tenser expression of his sister-in-law. The smile left his face. He and Wulfric exchanged brief glances, Wulfric's eyebrows lifting slightly.

"Is our food ready?" Sidroc asked, trying to ignore the tense atmosphere.

Gwyn gave her sister a final look and turned back to her kitchen area. "Soon. Be seated, and I will serve it."

Arietta met Wulfric's eyes, then quickly glanced away. There was a "biding my time" look about him that unsettled her.

Helga and Bjorn shuffled to their places on the bench, while Sidroc took his place at the center in his high seat. Gwyn placed the porridge, dried mutton, and buttermilk on the table before them, then seated herself at her husband's side.

Arietta hesitated. The only place left open to her was at Wulfric's side. He grinned in amusement at her indecision, somehow sensing her feelings. Lifting her chin slightly, she seated herself beside him, being very careful not to touch him in any way.

Although Arietta tried to ignore him, every time Wulfric handed her a bowl, he made a point of touching her hand. She became so nervous that she dropped the plate of mutton, watching its contents scatter across the wooden table.

Glaring at Wulfric's smug smile, Arietta apologized to Gwyn, then picked up the meat, returning it to the wooden plate and passing the plate to Bjorn. She avoided looking at anyone else, sure that they would all be staring at her.

After the meal was over, Wulfric got out his *hnefatafl* board and set it on the table. He looked at Arietta, his eyebrows raised. "Ready?"

Sidroc settled on one of the bunks, relaxing. After taking a much needed break, he and Wulfric would resume readying their equipment for the spring planting. He met his wife's eyes, and she rolled them at the ceiling, shaking her head. Grinning, he turned back to the game Wulfric and Arietta were playing.

Wulfric closed his palms over two of the pieces, one dark, the other light. Placing his hands behind his back, he then shifted them several times, holding them out to Arietta to choose.

Arietta's mouth went dry. It would be better to have the light pieces, for they were the most numerous and therefore one had a greater chance of capturing the other opponent's king. However, the one with the king got to move first, and with Wulfric's skill, that could be dangerous.

She tapped his left hand, and he turned over the light piece. Her relief was short lived when she glanced triumphantly into his eyes. They met hers with a full assurance of victory.

"Shall we make a wager?" he asked.

Arietta quickly shook her head negatively. "No, I think not. Games are meant for sport and enjoyment, not profit."

The provocative twinkle in his eyes increased her nervousness.

"As you wish," he murmured.

Wulfric set up the pieces on the nine-by-nine blocked board, then leaned forward to decide his first move. He slid one piece forward six spaces, then sat back, watching Arietta.

She was painfully aware of his close scrutiny and knew that it would muddle her ability to concentrate. Bjorn came and stood next to Wulfric, while Helga crawled into Arietta's lap. She snuggled the child close, feeling somewhat safer with the child as a shield between them.

After six moves, Arietta realized she was in serious trouble. Though Wulfric had started with only eight pieces and a king, he had managed to diminish her sixteen man force to half that size. Gnawing her lower lip with her teeth, she lifted her hand to move a piece, then hesitated.

Glancing up, she tried to discern if it would be a good move by Wulfric's face, but his features were closed and unreadable. Trying his own tactics, she leaned forward smiling provocatively and batting her eyelashes at him. His eyebrows flew up, then a slow smile curved his lips.

"It will not work, Arietta," he told her softly, his eyes dark and intense.

Her face filled with color, and she looked hastily away. It just wasn't in her to be wanton like Wendella. Moving the piece, she drew in a sharp breath when Wulfric quickly closed it in with a second piece, removing it from the board. Now she had only seven men left, to Wulfric's six. They were right when they said Wulfric was quite a master at this game. How had Wiglaf managed to defeat him?

Several plays later, Wulfric removed her final piece from the board. Arietta looked at him, swallowing hard at the profound look of victory on his face.

Bjorn shouted loudly at Wulfric's win, while Helga looked regretfully at her aunt. "He beat you," the child said sorrowfully.

"He certainly did," Sidroc said with a laugh. He smiled at Arietta apologetically. "But do not worry, Arietta. He is not invincible."

Arietta wasn't so certain.

"Just be glad you didn't wager with him," Gwyn reminded.

The morning quiet was suddenly pierced by the sharp sound of the warning horn. Three short blasts were followed by another three short blasts, then still others.

Wulfric was on his feet in an instant, as was Sidroc. Wulfric grabbed for his ax, while Sidroc reached for his sword. Together they ducked out the door.

Gwyn stood in the doorway, fear contorting her face. Arietta placed an arm around her shoulders, her own body trembling with terror. "Come, Gwyn. We must hide the children."

Gwyn shook her head. "No, if they are Norsemen, Sidroc, Wulfric, and the others will take care of them."

"We cannot take that chance," Arietta urged. "They are few against many."

Gwyn remained adamant. She closed the door and began clearing the table with shaking hands.

Arietta stood wavering between her desire to flee and her equally strong desire to stay. All her life she had been taught that the three horn blasts meant that the Norsemen were coming. Their ships were so fast that the villagers barely had time to flee before the Vikings would be upon them. There was no time for indecision.

But she couldn't leave her family. Not again. Determinedly, she took a seat, pulling Helga onto her lap and waiting for certain death—or worse.

❧

Wulfric topped the hill first, Sidroc right behind him. They skidded to a halt and stood looking down at the banks of the river as Norsemen jumped from their ship into the water and waded toward shore. Wulfric's voice rang out with warning. "Hold!"

At the sound of Wulfric's strong voice speaking their native tongue, the Norsemen glanced up in surprise. Their eyes went wide when they noticed the two hulking men standing just above them, their weapons at the ready. Before the invaders could react, Ingvar, Godfred, and others plunged from the forest in front of them.

Trying to be accepted by the villagers, some of the Norsemen had taken the English way of short hair and clean faces, but they were easily recognized by their girth. Swords and axes drawn, they faced the invaders boldly.

One man stepped forward from the ship, wading through the

turgid water. He was a giant, with flaming red hair and beard. Though he wore the fur vest of a Norseman, his pants were in the tunic style of the Moorish people. He lifted a hand in salute.

"My brothers," he shouted, his voice rumbling through the forest, "it is a joy to see you."

Wulfric and Sidroc slid down the hill to join the others. Sidroc stepped forward slightly, his frown fierce. "What are your intentions here, my brother?"

The giant held both hands out to the side, shrugging his shoulders. His laughter rang out boyishly. "We are here to trade with the English in this village, but if you have staked a claim on this land, then we will gladly trade with you."

Recognizing that the ship they were sailing was a trading vessel and not a warship, Sidroc relaxed slightly. Wulfric, however, stood tense and ready for anything that might occur.

The leader of the invaders stepped closer, stopping when Wulfric lifted his ax slightly. The leader's eyes met Wulfric's, and the other man stepped back quickly.

"They call me Rusbeard," he told Sidroc, still watching Wulfric carefully.

"I am Sidroc Ivarrson, and this is my brother, Wulfric."

A look of recognition passed through the man's eyes at the name. "You are sons of Ivarr of Hedeby?"

"We are," Wulfric agreed, his quiet voice losing none of its authority.

The other man smiled. "I have heard of you. Your reputation has spread far and wide."

Wulfric looked skeptical, but the other man lifted his eyebrows. "It is so. You are Wulfric who bested Askold of Trondheim in the games."

There was truth in what the trader said, but Wulfric remained dubious. When Rusbeard turned to his compatriots and commanded them to store their arms, the other men from the village relaxed slightly.

Rusbeard turned back to Sidroc. "Perhaps you have things you would like to trade?"

"Why are you here so late in the year? You will never make

it back to the north," Wulfric's suspicious eyes searched out each man.

"We are wintering on Lidasfarne."

Wulfric recognized the name of the island on the eastern portion of England. It was the very first place his people had landed when they'd begun their invasion of the area—a bloody time, and one he hoped would not be repeated. It would not do to anger King Alfred any further and destroy the fragile peace. But if these were men of trade, as they said they were, then they would already know that.

Rusbeard motioned to one of his men. The man quickly jumped aboard the ship, returning with a small chest. He threw it to Rusbeard, who caught it nimbly.

Opening the chest, he held it out for Sidroc's inspection. "Something for your wife perhaps?"

Sidroc ran his fingers through the small chest of jewelry. He lifted an amber necklace, the nuggets reminding him of his homeland where they rolled in from the sea on a regular basis.

Noticing his interest, Rusbeard smiled. "It is yours. Free of charge."

Sidroc glanced at him distrustfully.

"To show our goodwill and pure intentions," Rusbeard assured them. He smiled at Wulfric. "You choose something too, for your wife."

Wulfric took out a silver brooch for fastening a cloak at the shoulder. He clutched it tightly, testing its strength. Nodding at Rusbeard, he placed the item in his pouch.

As they continued to barter, tensions relaxed. Before long, the men mingled in familiar camaraderie. The invaders exchanged stories of their homeland, while the villagers shared their experiences on English soil.

Sidroc invited them to make camp on the shore of the river near their boat, but Wulfric made clear his warning when he advised the visitors to stay close to their ship.

When the villagers heard of the tradesmen, the shore came alive with people wanting to buy, sell, trade, or swap. The ealdorman came and made a pact with the foreigners that they could stay a fortnight. The whole area became like one great market, and with the festive atmosphere also came drinking and revelry.

ॐ

It was turning dusk when Arietta topped the rise to look on the scene below. She watched from afar, not certain that she wished to join the boisterous group. Wulfric saw her standing hesitantly on the fringes of the crowd and came to her. He held out his calloused hand in invitation. "Come. Join the party."

Arietta placed her hands firmly behind her back, quickly scanning the area to see if she could locate her sister and family. She did not miss Wulfric's lowering brows.

Aggravated, Wulfric took her by the forearm, dragging her along after him. "They are over here."

With the coming of night, the temperatures were rapidly dropping. A roaring bonfire was ignited using a chemical fire that the traders had brought with them. Arietta marveled at the incredible intensity of the flames that had burst into life in such a short period of time.

Off to the side, a smaller fire was lit. Men were laughing as they added small sticks to the blaze, kindling it into an even larger flame, yet careful to keep the flames burning low. Several Norsemen stripped to their waists, and several of the village men followed. Wulfric and Sidroc joined them.

"What are they doing?" Arietta asked her sister, huddling near the larger fire for warmth. "They will freeze like that."

Gwyn shook her head ruefully. "They are going to play Pull the Skin."

Arietta's eyebrows lifted slightly. "Play?"

"You will see."

When the fire was burning to the men's satisfaction, two groups formed, the village Norse on one side, the trading Norse on the other. They took hold of a long piece of leather skin, taking their places near the fire.

"The object is to pull one side into the fire," Gwyn told her, and Arietta could hear the dread in her voice.

"This is *play?*" Arietta's voice squeaked with surprise.

Rusbeard took his place at the head of his men, while Wulfric was chosen by the villagers to be the lead on their team.

The firelight from the bonfire lit the whole area around the crowd, but the light from the smaller fire shone on Wulfric's tense face. Arietta saw the same fierce concentration there that had been on his face earlier when they had played *hnefatafl*. He would not give up easily.

Rusbeard recognized the look as well. Eyes narrowed, a sudden grin split his face. He spit into his palms, rubbing them vigorously together, then picked up the hide.

Muscles played against muscles as each man strove to win the competition. Even in the chill air, sweat poured from their faces and chests. The teams were well matched, and the contest went on for some time before, with a cry that lifted the hair on the back of Arietta's neck, Wulfric gave a mighty pull, drawing Rusbeard into the blazing fire.

The other man came quickly out of the flames, patting his pants where small holes of scorched material smoked from the embers. His teammates, losing their advantage were thrown to the ground, some into the flames.

Arietta feared for Wulfric when the giant with the red hair faced him, but the other man laughed heartily, slapping Wulfric on the shoulder. Both Gwyn and Arietta sighed with relief.

Sidroc came and sat next to them, pulling his jerkin over his head. He grinned at his wife in unabashed pleasure. "We won."

"So I saw."

Arietta looked past Sidroc, expecting Wulfric to join them, but he was being borne off to a spot where a wrestling match was being held.

Gwyn frowned at her husband, but he shrugged good-naturedly. "He is a big boy. He can take care of himself."

Since Wulfric was otherwise occupied, Arietta decided that now would be the perfect time to leave this ostentatious show of male pride. She got to her feet, brushing down her skirt. "If you will excuse me, I think I will return to the village and see how Edwynn is doing. It seems everyone else is here."

Sidroc started to get to his feet. "I will walk with you."

Arietta shook her head, pushing him gently back to his place. "No, you stay here with Gwyn and the children. I will take a torch from the fire. I will be fine."

Sidroc would have argued, but Arietta did not give him time. Taking a burning stick from the fire, she made her way back to the village.

As she had supposed, Edwynn was lying alone in his hut. He turned his head when she entered, a small smile creasing his face.

"Hello," she called softly, dropping her torch into the fire and taking a seat at his side. "How are you today?"

"I am well," he responded, though he flinched with pain when he moved slightly to a sitting position. "Tell me what's happening."

"Viking traders. The whole village has turned out for the festivity."

She stopped suddenly, afraid that she might have offended him. He smiled ruefully.

"Except for me, you mean."

She nodded, and he shrugged. "That is fine with me. I have no desire to be with a motley crew of savages."

Since the entire village was involved, she thought that a poor assessment. Resolving not to argue with him, Arietta changed the subject. "I was told that Wendella has been caring for you today."

He shrugged again, turning his eyes away. "She feels indebted to me for her brother's life." He looked at her then. "Was she at the gathering too?"

Arietta nodded but refrained from telling him of Wendella's wild actions. If Edwynn truly did care for the girl, it would be painful for him to know how brazen she could be. In her mind, Arietta could still see the Norse girl floating from man to man, inviting their attention.

Arietta took Edwynn's hand, stroking it reassuringly like she would a child's. "Is there anything you would like me to get for you? Have you eaten?"

"I do not need anything. I am fine."

"Nothing?" Arietta teased, reaching forward to slide her fingers down his cheek. Her eyebrows lifted in surprise. "You have shaved!"

Color rose to his face, and he quickly glanced away. "Wendella did that for me."

Arietta noticed the tense set of his shoulders and wondered what had transpired between the two. "I did not think she would know how!"

The smile he gave her did not quite reach his eyes. "Norsemen may not shave, but they certainly know how to wield a knife."

He twisted Arietta's hand, pulling it against his chest. His eyes were serious, their normal sparkle swallowed up by some nameless worry. "Arietta, did you mean it when you said you would still marry me?"

Arietta felt her heart stop, then thunder on. She hoped that he wasn't suggesting what she thought he might be. "I meant it, Edwynn."

He tilted his head back on his pillow, staring up at the ceiling. "I have had a lot of time to think. There is no reason that I cannot farm and raise sheep. Other men have done so with greater disabilities than I have. I believe, after all, that I could take care of us."

Arietta had to force the words past the obstruction in her throat. "Of course you could. Did I not say so?"

Letting go of her hand, he wrapped his hand behind her neck and pulled her close until her face was mere inches from his. His eyes glittered strangely, and Arietta frowned, perplexed.

"Then I *will* marry you," he declared.

Several seconds went by before Arietta could answer him. She licked suddenly dry lips, striving to regain her composure. Before she could answer him, a deep voice interrupted him from the doorway. "I do not think so."

They both turned in surprise to find Wulfric standing at the open door.

ten

Edwynn struggled to rise, but Arietta firmly pushed him back against the bed. "Stay," she commanded in a voice which brooked no argument. She then turned her attention on the Norseman.

Wulfric stood glowering at them from the doorway, the planes and angles of his rugged face highlighted by the flaming torch he held aloft.

"You need to leave," she told him quietly. His dark-eyed look held denial, but Arietta refused to back down. He fixed Edwynn with a piercing glare. "I mean what I say."

Edwynn's face grew ruddy with anger. Arietta took a deep breath as Wulfric turned and left abruptly. She knew that if Wulfric had stayed another moment, Edwynn would have gotten to his feet to confront the unwelcome visitor.

Arietta crossed the room and closed the door against the cold. She leaned back against it, her gaze clashing with Edwynn's.

"I told you that he wanted you," he told her gruffly.

Arietta could no longer deny it. Whatever his reasoning, Wulfric seemed to have decided that she was the woman for him. The thought was so ludicrous, she almost laughed aloud. Only it was no laughing matter.

Straightening her back, Arietta hesitated. "I should go talk to him."

Edwynn snorted. "He did not look in any mood for conversation." He studied her carefully. "If you wish to be released from our bargain, I will understand."

Arietta's heart warmed at his concern. The smile she gave him barely curled her lips. "I meant what I said, also, Edwynn. I will not forsake you."

Edwynn's fingers curled into fists, and he glared at the ceiling. "I do not know what to do."

Arietta came back to him, her smile widening. She placed a cool hand on his forehead, brushing the hair from his eyes. Tilting her head slightly, she stared down at him until he finally turned her way.

"We will do whatever God wills us to," she said. "I will never break a vow that I made before God, Edwynn. You know that."

He took her hand, regarding her solemnly. "Arietta, could you learn to love me as a man?" he asked huskily.

Her insides turned to ice at the question. She fought a battle within herself but knew that she must be honest with him. "I do not know."

He continued to regard her, his mouth turning down at the corners. Finally he turned away from her, releasing her hand slowly. "You love him, do you not?"

Arietta sucked in her bottom lip, reluctant to bring the truth into the light. "Yes," she finally admitted.

Edwynn watched her knowingly. "And he wants you."

Arietta frowned. She went to the fire, prodding the burning coals into more life. She sat back on her heels, glancing at Edwynn over her shoulder. "That is not enough for me. Wants and desires fade with time. Besides, he is a heathen and refuses to be baptized."

"That means a lot to you, does it not?"

Arietta closed her eyes, her forehead puckering slightly. Her hands balled into fists in her lap. "It means everything."

Edwynn sighed. "Go to him, Arietta. Talk to him. If he will listen to you, then I release you from our agreement."

"I do not want to be released," Arietta told him softly.

"Arietta—"

"No," she interrupted forcefully, then lowered her voice. "Let us not speak of it again." She fixed him with a steely look. "I love you, Edwynn."

He nodded slightly, pulling the covers up to his chest. "But not like you love him."

"Nor like you love Wendella."

Edwynn flashed her an angry look.

Arietta got to her feet. "For the time being, concentrate on getting better." She crossed to the door and hesitated, her back to him. "We will speak more of this then."

When she left the hut, she wasn't surprised to find Wulfric waiting. She turned toward her own home, and he picked up his torch and fell into step beside her.

"You had no right, Wulfric."

His face was pinched with anger. "I have every right. I want you, and you want me. Is not that enough to give me the right?"

She stopped, turning to him in anger. "No. That is not enough." Her voice grew brittle with fury. "You want! I want! What about what *God* wants?"

He frowned, looking fierce in the glow from the flame he held aloft.

"What has your God to do with this?"

Arietta tried to fathom the look in his eyes but failed. She blew out a breath softly. "He has everything to do with this. He says that I must not be yoked together with an unbeliever." Her own eyes darkened considerably. "That is you, Wulfric. He gave it as a command, not as a suggestion. I will not disobey my Lord."

Wulfric's lips parted to speak, but no speech was forthcoming. He glared at her helplessly. "And if I accept this God of yours?"

Arietta's heart thrilled at the question, but then she realized what he was asking. Disappointment flooded through her. "You must accept him because you believe in Him, not for me."

"Then make me believe." The low comment was spoken with great force.

Arietta pushed the hair away from her face with frustration. "I do not know how," she answered bleakly. "I have not the wisdom."

He took her by the shoulders, his expression grim. "You have the words of the Holy One. Tell me about them."

She shivered in reaction to his nearness. He pulled her close, gently wrapping his arms around her and laying his cheek against her hair. Arietta slowly wound her arms around his waist.

"I want to understand," he whispered. "I want to know what makes you different from all other women I have ever known." He pulled back and looked into her face. Tears hovered on the rims of her lashes, and he brushed them away lightly.

"Not just for you," he gently chided, "but because if there really is one true God, then I want to know."

Her lips tilted slowly into a smile, and he brushed his fingertips across them, his look pensive.

"I will try," she said weakly. "Tomorrow."

She unwound her arms, pushing against him. He released her instantly, one brow lifted in question.

"Tomorrow," she reiterated.

Arietta could tell that Wulfric wasn't happy about the wait, but she needed time to organize her thoughts. This late in the evening, she was already tired, her mind foggy from tension.

Wulfric stopped at her gate, waiting until she entered her hut. They exchanged looks for a long time before Arietta finally closed the door between them.

❧

"What is repentance?" Wulfric demanded the next morning.

Arietta smiled. "Repentance means that you turn your back on your old life and promise to renounce your sins." Her breath blew out in frosty ringlets to match the whiteness on the trees of the forest that they were traipsing through. A morning songbird trilled from a tree close by, ignoring the frosty temperatures.

Wulfric frowned. "What sins?"

"All sins."

Wulfric came to a stop, leaning back against a boulder. He pulled Arietta between his outstretched legs, wrapping his arms lightly around her waist.

Arietta placed her hands firmly against his chest, her heart thundering in panic, but Wulfric merely contemplated her with a critical eye.

"What sins have you ever committed?" he gently asked.

"What do you consider a sin, Wulfric?" she countered.

The damp leaves on the ground crunched beneath his feet as he shifted position. He shrugged. "I do not know. Murdering someone without cause, I suppose. Unfaithfulness in a wife. Things like that."

Arietta leaned back against his encircling arms. "The Scriptures say that neither fornicators, nor idolaters, nor adulterers, nor homosexuals, nor male prostitutes, nor thieves, nor the covetous, nor drunkards, nor revilers, nor extortioners will inherit the kingdom of God."

Wulfric blew out a soft whistle. "Even drunkards will go to this hell of yours?"

Arietta almost laughed at Wulfric's bewildered look. "That is not all."

His blond brows lifted higher. "There is more?"

She nodded her head, suddenly enjoying herself. "Those who are full of hatred, who practice witchcraft, who are full of wrath, strife, uncleanness, lasciviousness, envy. . ."

He placed one large hand over her mouth. "Enough," he rebuked her darkly. "Is there anything left in your life to enjoy?"

She pulled his hand away and smiled into his eyes. "Oh yes, Wulfric. There is so much more."

"If a man cannot eat, drink, and be merry, then what is left but a hard life of toil, then death?"

Arietta stepped back from him, and he allowed her to leave the shelter of his arms. She turned and began walking toward the village. She glanced back at him and could feel her face warm with embarrassment as she said, "I suppose you mean by make merry, being with a woman."

He grinned, not denying it. She shook her head, rolling her eyes toward the sky. "God has always meant for one man and one woman to be together for life," she explained. "Marriage is a holy ordinance."

Wulfric stared speculatively at Arietta, and she felt uncomfortable under the intensity of his gaze. "And you really believe that a man who hates someone will go to the same hell as a man who murders someone?" he asked

"The Scripture says so," she agreed.

"And what does it say about marrying a man you do not love?" he asked softly.

Arietta tensed.

Wulfric once again pulled her to a stop. "What does it say, Arietta?" He lifted her chin with a curled forefinger, forcing her to look at him as she answered.

Arietta placed a hand on his wrist, her look wistful. "It says nothing about marrying a man you love, but it says that a wife must love her husband."

His eyes darkened. "And can you say that you will love Edwynn?"

"Yes, because the love it speaks of is a godly love. I already love Edwynn that way."

His nostrils flared, and he dropped his hand to his side.

"I made a vow," she declared, her eyes beseeching his for understanding. "The Scripture says much about keeping vows."

Wulfric's icy blue gaze fastened on her. "I make a vow to you, Arietta. I vow that you will never marry Edwynn as long as I am alive."

She opened her mouth to protest but was interrupted by a crashing in the forest to their right. Wulfric quickly pulled her behind him, his ax lifted and ready.

Rusbeard lumbered out of the trees, drawing up short when he noticed the two of them. Surprise gave way to delight on the man's face. "Wulfric! What ho! You left the festivities early last eve."

He noticed Arietta peeking out from behind Wulfric's back, and he came to a sudden stop. His mouth tilted slyly.

"But I can see why."

Frowning, Arietta looked at Wulfric. Since the other man spoke in Norse, she couldn't understand a word he said. She heartily wished that she could when Wulfric's face darkened with anger.

Rusbeard came closer, his eyes never leaving Arietta. Like Wulfric, he seemed to be obsessed with her hair, his eyes going over it time and again.

Arietta stepped to Wulfric's side and smiled hesitantly at the huge Viking. He doffed his cap, swinging it down as he bowed with a flourish. "My name is Rusbeard," he told her in perfect English.

Wulfric stood stoically by her side, his arms crossed over his chest. His attention was fixed steadily on the other man.

"I am Arietta."

The Viking lifted his gaze to Wulfric, his eyes gleaming. He spoke in Norse. "She would bring a fortune on the slave market."

Wulfric's eyes darkened with deadly intensity. "She is mine," he answered in the same language.

Wulfric's stance and features frightened Arietta. He looked as though he might very well kill someone. She frowned up at him. "What did he say?"

Wulfric's look never wavered from Rusbeard. The Viking held out his hands in supplication. He glanced at Arietta. "I said that you were a very beautiful woman."

Arietta's mouth dropped open, her face twisted with surprise. She let the falsehood pass without comment.

Rusbeard took his leave of them, looking back once. Wulfric stood watching him with extreme attentiveness. The other man grinned at Wulfric and disappeared into the forest. Arietta stared after him. She finally glanced up at Wulfric. "The Apostle John also says that all liars will go to hell."

Wulfric brought his attention back to her, grinning wryly. "It is the murder I am concerned with," he told her unequivocally, and Arietta's face paled.

They returned to Sidroc and Gwyn's home in silence, each absorbed by their own thoughts.

Arietta found Gwyn leaning over a bush outside their hut. She went quickly to her side, holding her hair away from her face while Gwyn continued to wretch.

Wulfric glanced from one to the other in concern. "Is she all right?"

Arietta's gaze brushed him briefly before she returned her attention quickly to her sister. "She will be fine. I will take care of her."

Looking relieved, Wulfric began backing away from them. "If you do not need me for anything, then I will go and find Sidroc."

Gwyn looked at him over her shoulder, her face and lips pale. "He is in the field," she croaked wanly.

Wulfric quickly departed, and Arietta helped Gwyn to the hut, grinning at the memory of Wulfric's alarmed face.

She helped Gwyn settle onto one of the sleeping benches, pulling a wolf pelt covering over her. Gwyn's face was covered with perspiration, and Arietta grew concerned.

"Helga," Gwyn protested, shivering beneath the blanket.

"I will find her," Arietta soothed. "And I will take care of her. You stay put until you feel better."

Gwyn nodded weakly, smiling in relief.

Arietta hovered near the doorway, not certain whether to go or stay. She finally went outside and found Helga sitting nearby. The little girl ran to Arietta, her eyes round with distress.

"Mutter is sick."

"Yes, I know."

Helga lifted her arms in entreaty, and Arietta picked her up. She smiled, chucking her niece under the chin. "How would you like to play a game of knucklebones?"

Helga placed one finger in her mouth, her blue eyes wide and winsome. "I do not know how."

"Well, then, I will have to teach you."

Arietta entered Gwyn's hut and found her sister already asleep. She sighed with relief, tucking the cover tightly about her shoulders. After stoking the fire, she carefully searched until she found what she was looking for, then she quickly returned outside.

She sat on the cold ground, and Helga huddled next to her. She showed Helga how to throw the pig's knuckles on the ground, keeping one to throw. Taking the knuckle she still held clutched in her hand, Arietta threw it into the air, grabbed another from the ground, then caught the thrown knuckle before it hit the ground.

Helga grinned with delight.

"Now, you try," Arietta suggested, handing Helga one of the knuckles.

It took Helga several turns before she finally was able to do it. She smiled in triumph.

Arietta returned her smile. "Now, we try it with two." She threw the two knuckles into the air, grabbing a third from the ground. Deftly, she caught them all.

Helga glanced from the pile to Arietta, her small face pinched with concern.

"It's all right, Helga. It takes time, but you can do it."

The two sat together for some time, their giggles ringing out around them. That was how Sidroc and Wulfric found them later.

When Helga saw her father, she squealed with delight and ran to him. He threw her high into the air, catching her with calm self-assurance. He grinned at Arietta, Helga held snugly in his arms.

"Where is Gwyn?"

Arietta glanced at Wulfric briefly but realized that he had said nothing to Sidroc of Gwyn's earlier bout with sickness. "She is resting."

Sidroc thrust his daughter into Wulfric's arms. He stepped over Arietta and hurried inside, the door banging behind him.

Bjorn settled next to his aunt on the ground, picking up the knucklebones. Wulfric glanced down at Arietta. "Another game?" he wanted to know.

She eyed him in challenge. "This one I could beat you at."

The light of combat instantly fired his eyes. He set Helga on the ground, bending to look at the knucklebones.

His look met Arietta's in defiance. "Shall we try?"

The door jerked opened, and Sidroc eyed them in panic. "Arietta, something is wrong."

Struck with terror, Arietta jumped to her feet and hurried after him. Gwyn lay moaning in pain on the bench, her head rolling back and forth in agony.

Arietta's terrified eyes met Sidroc's. "I will go for the midwife."

Sidroc barely acknowledged what she said, his attention already returned to his wife. Beads of sweat dotted his forehead; his eyes glittered with trepidation.

Arietta hurried outside. She found Wulfric sitting on a stump, Helga ensconced on his lap and Bjorn curled at his feet playing with the knucklebones.

Wulfric glanced up at her.

"I have to go for the midwife," Arietta told him. "Will you watch Helga and Bjorn?"

He frowned heavily. "I should come with you."

"There is no time," she argued. She dodged past him, running toward the village, fear lending wings to her feet. She banged on the midwife's door, and it opened slowly. An elderly woman peered out, her gray hair hanging in wisps about her wrinkled face.

"Arietta?"

"Oh Marta, can you please come?" Arietta begged, her breath coming in ragged gasps.

Puzzled, Marta looked behind Arietta. "Where?"

"My sister. Something is wrong."

Understanding flooded the old woman's features. "Let me get my cloak and bag."

Arietta danced impatiently from one foot to the other

while she waited in the cold. The afternoon sun was already on the descent, and it would soon be dark.

Marta hurried from her cottage, firmly closing her door behind her. She followed Arietta in as hurried a manner as she could, but Arietta still had to slow her pace considerably to allow the older woman to keep up.

When they reached the hut, Marta went inside, while Arietta waited with Wulfric and the children. The temperatures were dropping rapidly as the sky began to cover with clouds. Darkness would come even earlier to the land with the encroaching weather. Arietta squinted at the sky. "It is going to rain."

Wulfric nodded but said nothing.

"You should take the children to my house. They will be out of the weather there. We do not want them to get sick."

Wulfric's look scanned her face. "You need to come also."

Arietta shook her head firmly. "I cannot leave Gwyn."

"You cannot stay outside either," he refuted.

"I will not. When you leave, I will join Marta. I have helped her before."

Wulfric stood in indecision. His gaze rested on his niece and nephew briefly. He couldn't allow anything to happen to them. He also knew that he couldn't allow them to go inside their own house. It was far too early for Gwyn to deliver; therefore something must be seriously wrong.

He sighed, reaching down and lifting Helga into his arms. He looked at Arietta once, then commanded his nephew, "Come, Bjorn."

Bjorn went without hesitation.

Arietta entered the hut, wrinkling her nose at the smell of herbs and spices wafting in the air. She sat on the bench across from Gwyn, her glance going from her sister, to Sidroc to Marta. "How is she, Marta?"

Marta was pouring a drink into a cup. She took a burning tong from the fire and plunged it into the brew, nodding in satisfaction as the liquid hissed, the steam spiraling up from the cup.

"She has lost the child," Marta told her without preamble. "Now her body must rid itself of the child's body."

Arietta's heart dropped to her stomach. She looked at Sidroc sitting next to his wife, tears raining down his white cheeks.

"Will Gwyn live?" he croaked.

"Only the good Lord knows," Marta told him, lifting Gwyn's head and helping her to drink the brew.

Gwyn choked on the vile concoction, coughing and gagging. Marta allowed her patient's head to return to the pillow, brushing back strands of sweat-soaked hair.

"It will take a little time," she told them, glancing at Sidroc. "It would be best if you left."

Sidroc clenched his teeth, his eyes dark with pain. He shook his head. "No, I will stay with my wife."

Marta shrugged, pulling her shawl close about her. "As you wish."

Long minutes passed before Gwyn twisted and turned, writhing and screaming in pain. Sidroc turned terrified eyes to the older woman. "What have you done?"

Marta returned his look cooly. "It is time."

Arietta hovered nearby until it was finally over. Gwyn lay unconscious, her breathing steady but irregular.

Sidroc shoved his hands back through his hair, bowing in misery. "Dear God," he begged. "Let her live. Please let her live."

Arietta added her own petition to his. She wanted to comfort him, but she knew her words would not help.

"There is nothing more that I can do," Marta told them. "I need to return home and tend to my own."

Sidroc was obviously torn between the desire to see the woman safely home or staying with his wife. He glanced at Arietta helplessly.

Arietta got to her feet. "I will take her."

He shook his head vehemently. "No, you cannot go alone at night. I will have to go."

Arietta placed a hand on his shoulder, squeezing slightly. "I will be fine. Nothing happened to me last night, did it?"

Sidroc studied her in indecision. "Wulfric would kill me if anything happened to you. He would be upset to know that you traveled alone at night."

Arietta grinned wryly. "Let the wolf rage," she told him sardonically. "What he does not know will not hurt him."

Gwyn rolled her head, moaning. That action decided Sidroc. "So be it," he agreed reluctantly, dropping slowly to his seat.

Arietta grabbed her cloak and a torch from the fire, then followed Marta out the door. The night temperatures were below freezing. A light dusting of snow began to fall, and Arietta turned her free palm up, smiling slightly.

Marta smiled with her. "The first snow."

Arietta sighed. Something about snow always lifted her spirits, but not tonight. A tiny body awaited burial, and her heart ached both for Gwyn and for herself. The child would have been the first of Gwyn's family that Arietta had seen brought into the world, and she had been so looking forward to holding the tiny babe close. She lifted her face to the night sky, once again asking the Lord for Gwyn's life.

Arietta left Marta at her house and hurried back through the forest. She was halfway to Gwyn's house when someone stepped out of the trees.

Heart pounding with sudden fright, Arietta stopped.

"Who is there?" she called.

The figure stepped into the light of the torch, and Arietta recognized him instantly. "Rusbeard."

His slow smile upset her composure more than a little bit. "So," he greeted in English. "The little English siren."

The look in his eyes warned Arietta. She began backing away, but Rusbeard followed.

"I have plans for you," he told her, his voice sending warning tingles up her back. "I have followed you all day hoping for a chance to see you without your protector."

It finally dawned on Arietta that she had been foolish to roam through the woods at night alone, especially with a ship of Vikings nearby.

Arietta turned to run, but Rusbeard was upon her before she had taken two steps. He threw a woven sack over her head, lifting her over his shoulders.

Though Arietta kicked and screamed, she couldn't make him release her. As he trudged through the night forest, the steadily falling snow swallowed his tracks behind him.

eleven

Wulfric lay his now sleeping nephew next to his already sleeping niece. He threw the blanket over the two and quietly left the room.

The flames in the fire pit were still blazing after his careful tending. He sat down on the floor next to the pit, brushing his tired face with his hands. He leaned back against the bench, closing his eyes and allowing the thoughts that he had so carefully held at bay to flock into his weary mind.

His mind centered on Gwyn and the possible loss of her child. It was the Viking way to accept such things without much thought or grief. Among his people, children could be thrown into the river if a father did not want them or even if there were too many mouths to feed, but such was not Gwyn's way. Nor his, for that matter.

He had always considered life sacred, something not to be taken lightly. Where he had gotten his ideas he wasn't certain. Perhaps it was from the priest who had first visited his people so many years ago. He had been a gentle man, kind and considerate. The Norsemen had laughed at him, but he still treated them with love and respect. This had eventually won the priest many converts, though later he had been slain by followers of Odin.

Wulfric's father had been converted to Christianity by the man, and his mother had divorced him soon after. Wulfric could barely remember her, but what he did remember was not to his liking. She had been harsh and unloving, nothing like Gwyn. Nor Arietta, for that matter.

Over the past few weeks, Arietta had made a point of trying to befriend Wendella and Godfred. Godfred was quick to succumb to her gentle charm, but Wendella was a somewhat

different story. Truth to tell though, Wulfric had seen a softening in Wendella of late that he had never expected to see.
When she looked at Arietta, a hungry light filled her eyes,
mixed with a good degree of scorn. A battle waged within
Wendella, that was for certain, and he looked forward to seeing which side of her nature would win.

Lifting his eyes to the ceiling, he allowed his thoughts to
roam to the discussion that he and Arietta had had that morning. Could he truly give up so much, and to what purpose?
Yet did Arietta lack for anything? She was fed and clothed,
happily helping others who had much less, some more.
Arietta was just happy helping, and that was the end of it.

She was so full of goodness and love, her eyes filled with
innocent wonder. There was something so untouchable
about her it made it a challenge for any man to see if he could
win her.

Wulfric's eyes began to gleam with his thoughts. Though
Arietta might deny it, he knew that she was his. They be-
longed together. The problem was getting her to see that.

His blood began to heat when he thought of her response to
his kisses. She had become aware of him as a man, and she
had reacted with surprising passion. At the same time, he had
never known a woman who could so instantly go from fire to
ice. And her God was at the center of it, he was certain.

Was it wrong for a man to take pleasure with a woman?
When he tried to summon to mind other women he had
known, he found even thinking of them in the same breath as
Arietta left a sour taste in his mouth. Was this love?

He stirred the fire gently, his mind still far away. Arietta
had spoken of being in love with the Lord. He suddenly realized how she must feel loving her Lord the way she did and
being faced with other gods. She was committed to one God
for life, just as she said it was meant for a man and woman.
Anything else in her mind was tantamount to adultery.

The thought of one mate for life loomed suddenly favor-
able within him. He yearned for a loving relationship such as

Sidroc and Gwyn had. A gentle love that still had fire to it.

He got up suddenly and went into the kitchen area, grabbing a hunk of goat's cheese from the table. As he nibbled, thoughts continued to swirl unendingly through his head.

What was his purpose in life? There had to be more than feeding the flesh and stealing and killing. Why did he feel so empty when living that life, yet so fulfilled when he shared with others like Wiglaf and Martha? What was it Arietta had said? That God's law could be summed up in two statements: Love the Lord with all your heart, mind, soul, and body; and love your neighbor as yourself.

By practicing such a thing, he had found fulfillment beyond his wildest imaginings. Did that then make Arietta's God the true God? Was there truly only one God, and did He truly desire Wulfric's submission to His will to enter into eternity with Him? The place Arietta described had started a yearning deep inside him. He wanted to be in that beautiful place, and if it meant giving his life to this God, then so be it. Thor, Odin, and Frey had done nothing for him but cause misery. And Valhalla promised only eternal drinking sprees, eternal fighting, and an eternity of satiating one's lust. Her heaven sounded infinitely better.

A sudden pounding on the door interrupted his revery. He quickly crossed the room, trying to reach the door before the person on the other side could awaken the children. When he jerked open the door, he found Ingvar standing there, a dark frown drawing down his face.

"Wulfric, Sidroc told me that I could find you here."

Wulfric opened the door wider. "Come in."

Ingvar shook his head. "No. I have come to tell you that I decided to go with the traders as far as the Danelaw."

"I see." Wulfric's smile was without humor. "Come in anyway."

Again Ingvar shook his head. "No. What I wanted to tell you was that I was coming back to the village to tell you and the others good-bye, but when I reached the edge of the forest,

Rusbeard came out the other side. He did not see me, but I saw him. He was carrying something over his shoulder."

Wulfric's interest quickened. "What was it?"

"Your woman."

Wulfric's eyes widened, the blood congealing in his veins. Suddenly, his adrenalin began to flow in a swift flood tide, a fever beginning to burn in his blood. He grabbed for his ax and started to pass Ingvar, but then remembered the children. He turned to Ingvar.

"Ask Wendella to come here to stay with the children, and tell Godfred to come to the river."

Ingvar grabbed his arm. "You had better hurry. They were making ready to cast off."

Wulfric looked deep into his eyes. Recognizing the other man's loyalty, he clasped Ingvar's shoulder. "Thank you, Ingvar."

Wulfric ran toward the river, his fear for Arietta driving him forward without thought to safety. He skimmed fallen trees, ignoring the gorse bushes that tore at his leggings. Though his breath rose in frosty circles around him, he was immune to the biting cold.

He plunged out of the forest just beyond the river and came to an abrupt halt. The Norse ship was just where it had been anchored, the crew moving quickly about the area in preparation for departure. A huge bonfire blazed near the ship, lighting the surrounding area for quite some distance.

Arietta sat on the ship, her arms tied tightly to her sides. In a brief glance, he could see that she was well, though her eyes were shining with fear. Some of the terror that had gripped him faded, but his anger intensified so that he saw Rusbeard through a red haze.

Before Wulfric could act, Arietta got to her feet and plunged head first into the freezing water, submerging below the dark surface. Wulfric started forward, but Rusbeard reached into the river and laughingly pulled Arietta out of the water.

She struggled against his hold, lashing out with the one

weapon available to her: her teeth. Rusbeard lifted his hand to strike her when, with unerring accuracy, Wulfric tossed his ax into the air and sent the instrument flying to embed itself in the ship's hull, mere inches from Rusbeard's face.

All motion ceased on the ship as the crewmen tried to locate the intruder. One man shouted, pointing at Wulfric's still form.

Rusbeard turned slowly to face Wulfric, still holding Arietta firmly in his arms. He handed her squirming body up to one of his men in the ship and quickly pulled the ax from the hull, turning to face Wulfric.

Though weaponless, Wulfric felt no fear. His anger had driven him beyond reason. He started walking toward Rusbeard, his hands clenching into fists at his side.

Wulfric heard a commotion behind him and turned to find Godfred and Ingvar mere feet away. Both men had their eyes on Rusbeard.

Godfred pulled the ax from his belt and hefted it to Wulfric, pulling his sword from its sheath at the same time.

Wulfric caught the ax with ease, turning to once again face his foe.

Rusbeard paused, eyeing the three men. He smiled slowly, holding his arms out to his sides. "Come, my friends," he implored. "Let us reason together. The woman will fetch a high price on the slave market, and I am willing to share. I will even allow you any of my trade goods in exchange. We could both make a profit from this."

"Any profit you have, you will not live long enough to spend," Wulfric answered, his steel-edged voice causing the other man's face to drain of color.

Nonetheless, Rusbeard spoke with bravado. "There are three of you, Wulfric, and fifteen of us." He lifted an eyebrow. "And we are all Viking."

Wulfric did not miss the threat.

"You are wrong, Rusbeard," another voice answered. "There are more of us."

Other Norsemen came from the woods, their axes and swords gleaming in the light from the fire. Wulfric turned back to Rusbeard. "Let the woman go."

Rusbeard stood in indecision. His men awaited his decision. With sudden determination, he turned to the man holding Arietta. "Untie her."

The man quickly did so. He helped Arietta over the side of the ship, releasing her as soon as she found her feet in the water.

Arietta waded ashore, her angry glare settling on Rusbeard as she passed him. He shrugged, giving her a broad smile. Pulling Wulfric's ax from the ship, he turned and hurled it toward Wulfric. It sliced into the frozen ground at his feet. Wulfric stood unmoving, his arms folded across his chest and his eyes never leaving the trader.

When Arietta reached the bank, she clawed her way up the muddy sides until she could finally get her footing. She trudged her way to Wulfric's side, her soaking dress slogging around her ankles.

Wulfric pulled her behind him, still facing the trader. Rusbeard looked past Wulfric to Ingvar. "You are still welcome to come with us."

Ingvar hesitated, his look going from Wulfric to Rusbeard. "I think that I will wait."

"As you wish."

The trader turned, making a sign that his men understood. They quickly loaded the rest of the supplies and climbed aboard the ship.

After Rusbeard lifted himself aboard, he turned back to the shore. Lifting his hand in a friendly wave, he told them, "Perhaps we will see you again."

Godfred glowered at him. "That would not be wise. We will do our trading elsewhere."

Barking an order at his men, Rusbeard shrugged with good humor as the ship quickly moved away from the cove. His hearty laugh rang out behind him, echoing through the forest.

When the ship was far enough away, Wulfric lifted his ax and turned to Arietta. "Are you all right?"

She stood shivering with cold, her arms wrapped tightly around her and her teeth chattering loudly enough for everyone to hear. "I am–m–m f–f–fine."

"We must get her home," Godfred interjected.

Wulfric shouted something at the others in Norse, and laughing loudly, they nodded their heads and suddenly melted out of sight. Arietta stood staring after them open mouthed. How could people so large just disappear as if they had never been?

Wulfric lifted her into his arms and, when she would have protested, shushed her with a quick kiss.

"Be still. I will return you to Gwyn's."

Feeling the warmth of his body seeping into her freezing extremities, she subsided. Cuddling closer, she nudged her head into the hollow of Wulfric's neck. She heard his quick intake of breath and smiled slightly to herself.

With Wulfric's long stride, it did not take them long to reach the hut. He thumped on the door, and Sidroc opened it. His eyes went wide at sight of Arietta's dripping form held close in Wulfric's arms.

"What happened? Ingvar came here to find you, and he was extremely upset. He would not tell me what was wrong."

Wulfric pushed past him, setting Arietta next to the blazing fire.

"Rusbeard decided to leave tonight, and he decided that Arietta would make a fine prize on the slave market."

Sidroc's shocked look fixed on his sister-in-law. "What?"

"It is a long story," Wulfric told him. "I will tell you everything after Arietta gets out of her wet clothing and into something drier."

Arietta was staring at her sister's still form, unable to voice the question she wanted to ask for the fear that clogged her throat. She finally managed to croak out, "How is Gwyn?"

Sidroc's tender gaze focused on his wife. "She is alive. She awakened some time ago but then went back to sleep. I think she will be all right."

Arietta hoped that he was right. Sidroc and Wulfric turned their backs to her, and she hastened out of her freezing wet clothing. Quickly wrapping a blanket around her, she huddled shivering near the fire, her thoughts chaotic.

She wanted to go to Gwyn but saw Sidroc hovering near her side. That was his place, not hers. She glanced up at Wulfric, and unexpectedly, he gave her a smile of understanding.

While Sidroc tended his wife, Wulfric cared for Arietta. He brought her a hot, herbal drink and encouraged her to drink it. She wrinkled her nose with distaste but did as he suggested, knowing the herbs would help prevent illness after her exposure to cold.

Sidroc looked at his brother. "Where are Bjorn and Helga?"

"Wendella is with them. I will get them soon, if you think that it is all right to return them here."

Sidroc studied his wife's sleeping face, reaching out to brush a damp strand of hair from her forehead. "Let us wait until the morrow."

Wulfric nodded. "As you wish. I will ask Wendella to stay with them until tomorrow." He lifted a brow in Arietta's direction. "I will bring you some dry clothes if you will tell me where to find them."

Arietta did so, and Wulfric opened the door and left. After he was gone, an eerie silence pervaded the room. Shadows caused by the firelight's flickering flames danced around the still room. It was some time before Sidroc spoke. "I am sorry, Arietta. If anything had happened to you, it would have been my fault."

Surprised, Arietta turned to him. "That is not so. You could not have known that Rusbeard would commit such an act."

Sidroc's sky blue eyes darkened to turquoise. "I knew that I should not let you go alone."

Arietta sighed softly. "Sidroc, you had no choice. It was either me or Marta."

Smiling wryly, Sidroc allowed his look to pass over Arietta briefly. "Somehow, I do not think that Marta would have had such a problem."

Arietta blushed, turning away from Sidroc's close scrutiny and stirring the fire with an iron prong.

Time passed slowly until the door opened, and Wulfric entered. He handed Arietta a bundle of clothing and seated himself close to his brother. Arietta quickly changed into her dry clothes, sighing with relief from the bone chilling cold.

Gwyn's breathing rose and fell rhythmically, letting them know that for the time being all was well. The three settled down to a long night's vigil.

Wulfric glanced at Arietta. "I believe you challenged me to a game of knucklebones earlier."

Arietta knew that he was only trying to get her mind off the dark possibilities looming ahead of them. Her smile was forced. "Do you know how to play?"

He grinned back at her. "I have a fair idea."

She swiftly rose to her feet. "I forgot the knucklebones outside."

Wulfric got up, motioning her to stay put. "I will get them."

When he returned, the two of them settled down to play the game. Arietta apprized him of the rules and watched in amazement at his quick dexterity in catching the bones. In the end, they were evenly matched, and the game ended in a tie.

Wulfric tilted his head, a small smile tugging at his lips. "Perhaps you would prefer another game of *hnefatafl*."

"I think that I will wait until my mind is able to focus on the game," Arietta told him dryly, giving him a searing look, and he laughed.

Sidroc watched their banter, a half-smile playing about his lips. He said something to Wulfric in Norse, and Wulfric's eyes fastened on Arietta. Wulfric softly answered him, and both men continued staring at her.

She glared from one to the other. "What are you saying?"

Sidroc lifted a hand in a placating gesture. "Nothing

important." He then deftly changed the subject. "Arietta, will you share with us more of God's Word?"

Taken aback, Arietta opened her mouth twice before she could finally speak. "What would you like to know?"

Wulfric answered for him. "Everything."

He handed Arietta a blanket, and she gratefully accepted it. Snuggling down under its warmth, she turned her attention to the two men.

"I will do my best," she told them uncertainly and decided to start with the creation of the world. Both men quietly listened to her, interjecting questions periodically. Their intent looks somewhat unnerved her, but she stumbled along with her story.

When she came to the part of Jesus' death on the cross, her eyes filled with tears, her voice filled with deep-felt passion.

"Why would your God allow His own Son to die for those who do not even love Him?" Wulfric asked in anger. "That makes no sense."

"God is so sinless," she told him fervently, "that He cannot look on the sins of others. For Him to be able to see past our sins, He must be able to see us sinless."

Wulfric shook his head. "That is impossible."

"Without the Lord Jesus, you would be correct. But when He died on the cross, when He shed His blood for our sins, His very blood formed the veil that He sees us through. God is able to see us through Jesus' blood as sinless."

Frowning, Wulfric glanced at his brother. Sidroc shrugged.

"I still do not see how that is possible," Wulfric told her.

Arietta leaned back against the bench, her mind growing fuzzy with fatigue. "Truth to tell," she told them, "I do not fully understand it myself. I only know that by faith I accept it as truth."

She yawned widely, and Wulfric grinned at his brother.

"I think she is bored with our company."

Arietta tried to assure them otherwise, but Sidroc laughed away her efforts. "My brother was only teasing you. Why don't you choose a bench and get some sleep? I will awaken you if anything untoward happens."

Arietta's first thought was to reject such an idea, but after the day's events, she was thoroughly exhausted. Nodding at Sidroc, she chose a bench close to Gwyn, yet far enough away to afford her some privacy.

She was thankful when Wulfric added another blanket to the one she had already clutched around her. Her body had yet to recover from the icy river. She only hoped that she would not become ill. Someone was going to have to take over for Gwyn.

When Arietta's lashes fanned across her cheeks, and her breathing became regular, Wulfric relaxed. He looked at Sidroc. "I need some exercise. I will cut some more wood for the fire."

Sidroc understood. "You could have killed Rusbeard. Why did you not do so?"

Wulfric's look rested briefly on Arietta. "It did not seem the thing to do."

Crossing his arms over his chest, Sidroc leaned back in his seat, staring fixedly at his brother. He spoke in Norse. "So, she has managed to tame you."

Wulfric did not deny it. "I am not certain if it is the woman herself or the words she speaks. It would be nice to believe in such a place as this heaven." He looked at Sidroc. "Do you?"

Sidroc shrugged. "It takes faith, as Arietta says. I am not certain that I possess such faith myself."

"I heard you praying to this God for Gwyn," Wulfric argued. "You must have *some* faith."

Again, Sidroc shrugged. "I only asked because I did not know where else to turn."

Wulfric lifted a brow. "Why did you not appeal to Odin? Or Thor? Or Frey?"

Sidroc had no answer. Wulfric clapped him on the shoulder as he passed him. "I think in your heart you know."

At Sidroc's call, Wulfric turned back from the door.

"Do you, Wulfric?"

Wulfric glanced across at the sleeping Arietta. "I am not certain."

Sidroc nodded understandingly, and Wulfric retreated into the frosty night air. His thoughts roamed the same road they had earlier, treading down to a fine path. And that path led in a definite circle.

He picked up the ax and began chopping the wood. With each downward stroke, some of the tension left his body.

Arietta was safe, and he could relax and try to forget the feelings of intense hatred that had flashed through his body when he had faced Rusbeard. It was disquieting when such killing thoughts came to mind to have them suddenly ousted by words that Arietta had spoken. *Murderers will go to hell.*

This hell that Arietta described was not something he would wish to visit, much less spend an eternity there. But did he really believe all that she said?

According to the Christians, God had left His Word in book form so that everyone could hear it. Such was not the case with the Norse gods. And while Arietta claimed her God was eternal, that too was not the case with the Norse gods. According to legend, in the end they would be destroyed as well as all of mankind.

More and more, the thought of a peaceful eternity appealed to him. What Christianity had to offer was by far more alluring than any of the other religions he had encountered on his travels.

He carried the wood to the house, stacking it against the hut. Peeking his head in the door, he told his brother, "I am going to the village to check on Bjorn and Helga."

Sidroc looked relieved. "I would appreciate that."

It took Wulfric no time to reach the village. Everything lay quiet and peaceful in the frosty morning air. Dawn was already breaking over the horizon. Soon, the whole village would be alive with activity, but right now it was hushed and still.

He made his way to Arietta's house, rosy fingers of pink

light highlighting the daub and wattle walls as the sun continued to rise.

He knocked on the door, and Wendella opened it too quickly for her to have been unaware of his presence. Her lips curled into an alluring smile. Wulfric heaved a silent sigh, fully aware of her tactics. He had hated to ask her to watch the children in the first place, knowing that she would use the favor against him. The look in her eyes last night had told him so.

"Come in," she told him, motioning behind her.

Wulfric remained where he was. "I cannot. I must return home quickly, but I wanted to see how Bjorn and Helga were."

She opened the door wider. "Come in and see for yourself."

Wulfric tried to squelch his rising irritation. "Are they asleep?"

Wendella narrowed her eyes. "Yes, they are."

"Then I do not wish to disturb them," Wulfric told her and tightened his lips. He turned to go, but Wendella placed a hand on his arm. Her cool fingers slid across his forearm, yet her touch left him unmoved.

"What happened last night? Is Godfred all right?"

Wulfric let down his guard at her genuine concern for her brother. It was the one thing that always caused Wulfric to hold her in some favor. There was no one on this earth that Wendella loved more than Godfred, not even herself.

"He is well," he assured her. "There was no fighting."

Something flashed briefly through her eyes that Wulfric could not interpret.

"And Arietta?"

Wulfric studied her falsely anxious face, frowning slightly. "She is well also. She is at home with her sister. Gwyn lost the child."

Wendella's mouth dropped open, her face contrite. "I am sorry to hear that."

She truly seemed distressed, and Wulfric nodded. He turned to go, and this time she allowed him to leave. He had just reached the gate when they heard a shout from the end of the village.

"House on fire!"

Wulfric tried to see from which house the smoke was issuing. Wendella joined him at the gate, her anxious gaze peering in the same direction.

"That is the direction of our house," she said under her breath.

Other villagers started hurrying past, hoping to stem the tide of the flames and thus spare any other home from destruction.

Wendella's eyes grew wider as the flames rose higher. "It *is* our hut! Godfred is there alone!"

Before Wulfric could stop her, she rushed out the gate and ran toward the billowing smoke. He hesitated but knew he could not leave the children alone. He watched transfixed as the crowd formed around the burning house, but he could make out no distinct figures. Where were Godfred and Wendella?

A shrill scream froze Wulfric's insides. He recognized it instantly as Wendella's.

"What is happening, Uncle Wulfric?"

Wulfric turned to find Bjorn regarding him from the doorway. His sleepy eyes blinked at his uncle in question.

"Bjorn," Wulfric told him harshly. "Stay here and watch your sister. Do not let her out of your sight. Do you hear me?"

Bjorn's eyes lost all signs of sleep. They widened perceptibly, and he nodded.

Wulfric jumped the gate, running to the end of the village. The villagers were trying to throw buckets of water on the blazing house, but everyone could sense the futility of the gesture.

Wulfric pushed his way forward. He noticed one of his fellow Norsemen standing nearby.

"Sveyn, where are Godfred and Wendella?"

"In there," the other man told Wulfric grimly.

Horrified, Wulfric turned to the blazing inferno. Without thinking, he plunged through the doorway and into the flames.

He stumbled over Wendella's body, lying at his feet. She had Godfred clutched by the arm and had obviously dragged him across the floor toward the door. The smoke must have gotten to her before she could get him outside.

The flames drew closer, singeing the hair on Wulfric's legs and arms. Reaching down, he picked Wendella up in his arms. The flames engulfed the door. Taking a deep breath, he plunged through the wall of flame.

Ingvar was just outside the door. He took Wendella from Wulfric, while Sveyn put out the flames igniting Wulfric's clothes.

Wulfric turned back to the hut, but Sveyn reached out to stop him.

"You cannot go back in there."

Wulfric shrugged off his hand. "I have to. Godfred is still in there."

Everyone watched in horror as Wulfric once again plunged through the flames, only to appear moments later with Godfred in his arms.

Again, Sveyn doused the flames on Wulfric's clothes. His trousers, vest, and shirt were now dotted with scorched holes.

Ignoring the burns on his skin, Wulfric knelt beside Godfred. He felt for a pulse but could find none. Leaning back, Wulfric closed his eyes in anguish. Godfred had been like a brother to him, and now he was gone.

He turned to Wendella, lying beside her brother, and gasped, appalled by the sight that met his eyes. One side of her face was burned badly, the hair on that side of her head charred to a slight nub. Her arms too had bad burns. She would be scarred for life if she lived, her beauty gone forever. Wulfric felt for a pulse, almost hoping that he would not find one. But he did. It beat faintly, but it beat nonetheless.

twelve

Arietta stood beside Sidroc on the hill overlooking the river. The Viking long ship that had brought Godfred into their lives, now stood ready to help him depart into eternity. Fog swirled eerily about the ship, its dragon's head peering out through patches of mist.

Wulfric had been chosen to set fire to the ship with God-fred's body resting on board. Though Godfred had claimed Christianity, many of his compatriots had not, including Wendella. It had been the one bone of contention that stood between them over the past weeks.

Now, for their sakes, Ingvar had agreed to give up the idea of sailing to Iceland and had suggested that they use the ship as a final farewell to both Godfred and their dreams of a new settlement in the icy waters of the north.

Wulfric stood to the side, holding a torch and awaiting the signal to light the fire. Others moved back and forth through the mist, crossing the cove to add items to the ship that they felt Godfred would need in the afterlife.

Arietta watched the eerie scene, her heart hollow with sadness. She had grown fond of Godfred over the past weeks, and now she would miss their long conversations about the Scriptures. She pulled her cloak tightly about her, trying to ward off some of the winter's chill.

Slaughtered animals were added to the growing pile of items awaiting their turn to burn in the funeral pyre. She swallowed hard, thankful that Godfred had accepted Christianity and would not need these items, thoughtful though they were.

Sidroc glanced down at her, lines etched wearily across his face. His grim countenance held both contempt and acceptance. It was the way of his people and one they would not give up easily. Especially among those who were forced to accept Christianity yet held to their reverence for the Norse gods.

When all was ready, everyone stepped back to allow Wulfric passage. He looked up at Sidroc standing above him and nodded briefly. Sidroc returned his nod, glancing down at the small bundle resting in his arms. He moved forward, making his way down the small hill and across to the ship.

Arietta's heart began to beat more quickly. Sidroc was the child's father and had every right to do as he wished with the small body, but Arietta felt that it would have been best buried among her people where Gwyn would be able to visit the small grave from time to time. She had mentioned this to Sidroc, but he had been adamant.

She watched as Sidroc laid the small bundle across Godfred's chest and wrapped the Norseman's arms around it to hold it safely in place. He stepped back from the ship, his eyes glistening with unshed tears, and Arietta knew that they were for both his lost child and his best friend.

She couldn't hear the words spoken by the others, but it was a signal for Wulfric to step forward and set light to the piled kindling. As the ship became engulfed in flames, its moors were released and it floated out onto the river, the current carrying it beyond the shore and into the thickening fog beyond.

Wulfric climbed the hill to stand at her side, almost as though he knew how emotionally devastating the whole ordeal was to her. As the flames encased the bodies, Arietta turned away, a small choking sound escaping her throat. Wulfric pulled her into his arms, and she did not resist him. She felt his warmth surround her like the summer sun, making her feel safe for the first time in days.

The tears that she had held at bay now forced their way out of her eyes, leaving icy trails down her cold cheeks. Wulfric brushed them away with a large thumb, holding her even closer while he continued to watch the burning ship.

Ingvar came to stand beside them, his voice filled with satisfaction. "He will go quickly to Valhalla, now. I am glad that we chose to burn the ship. Better he arrive in Valhalla quickly, than to spend a long time getting there after being buried."

Wulfric said nothing. If what Arietta said was true, then something called angels had taken Godfred to Abraham's bosom like a man named Lazarus. He wished that he could truly believe in such things, but his logical mind was having a hard time accepting them. Still, his emotional side had been awakened in the past few months, and that side wanted so much to believe. He now understood the dilemma that Wendella was experiencing.

He only hoped that Wendella would have time to sort things out. As it was, she lay unconscious in Arietta's house, and they did not know if she would revive. Again, he almost hoped that she would not. For someone like Wendella, losing her beauty would be worse than losing her soul.

He had asked a villager to sit with Wendella while he attended Godfred's funeral. Now he needed to make his way back to her. For some reason he felt extremely responsible for her condition, though he knew that such feelings were illogical.

Ingvar left with the others, and Sidroc joined Wulfric and Arietta. He glanced at Arietta held close in Wulfric's arms but said nothing.

Wulfric felt his brother's intent perusal and chose to ignore it. "How is Gwyn today?"

Sidroc sighed wearily, his breath forming a frosty fog around his face. "She is weak, but she seems to be recovering. I have not told her about Godfred yet."

Wulfric nodded. "That is probably wise."

Arietta pushed out of Wulfric's arms, wiping her tears with the back of her hand. Her forlorn face was pinched with grief. "I must go to her."

"What about the children?" Wulfric queried. "I think I should bring them home now. It would not be wise to allow them to see Wendella. The sight might frighten them."

Arietta frowned, clutching her cloak with frozen fingers. "Is she truly as bad as that?"

Wulfric answered with a look.

"Bring them," Sidroc directed. "Gwyn needs to have her children around her." He then took Arietta by the arm, and they turned toward the path that led through the forest to Sidroc's house. Wulfric turned to watch them until they were out of sight.

When Wulfric brought the children home later, they were subdued, but excitement simmered just under the surface. Though Wulfric managed to get them to quietly open the door, once inside, their true personalities reappeared. Their eyes shone with the excitement and fun of the adventure of being with their uncle. They were far too young to understand the tragedy that had struck this house.

The dark emptiness left Gwyn's eyes when her children surrounded her with their bubbling personalities. She hugged them tightly, her eyes brimming with tears. Both pulled back from her bewildered, Bjorn frowning with annoyance. Helga on the other hand, quickly took the opportunity to climb up beside her mother on the sleeping bench.

Sidroc went to move her away, but Gwyn motioned him away. With shaking hands, she brushed her matted hair away from her face. She turned her white face to Helga, smiling into her daughter's bright eyes.

"Tell me about your night."

So Helga proceeded to do so.

Wulfric watched them, a tight knot forming in his throat. Gwyn was strong. She would survive, as she had before, but he wondered why life had to be so hard. He turned away, encountering Arietta's steadfast gaze. She gave him a sympathetic smile.

He picked up his ax and turned to his brother.

"I must go. Someone needs to stay with Wendella."

"I will come too," Arietta told him, reaching for her cloak.

Wulfric frowned. "But you are needed here."

Arietta's look went over the little family. She knew that Gwyn would want time to be alone with them, time to heal a broken heart. Gwyn lifted sad eyes to Arietta, and Arietta's face softened with love. They understood each other. They always had.

"I will return later. Right now, I would like to check on Wendella."

Wulfric didn't argue further. He opened the door and allowed Arietta to proceed him out into the cold. They walked in silence for some time, both busy with their own thoughts. The fog had burned away with the morning sun, leaving the trails clear.

Wulfric suddenly pulled Arietta to a stop, shushing her with a hand laid gently on her mouth. He pointed in the distance, and following the direction of his pointing finger, Arietta saw a small roe deer standing just inside the forest. It stood with its ears twitching, its nose testing the air.

Arietta became absolutely still. They both watched the little animal for some time before something alerted it, and it bounded off into the thick trees. Arietta smiled up at Wulfric, her eyes shimmering with delight.

Wulfric's lips tilted ruefully. He wasn't about to spoil her pleasure by suggesting that his reason for stopping had been to slay the animal for their supper that night. Her face filled with pleasure, and wonder had stopped him.

Their brief interlude helped to break the silence, and both chatted agreeably while they finished walking the distance to the village.

Arietta entered the house, followed by Wulfric. A young woman rose to her feet, and Arietta recognized her as the combmaker's daughter. The girl's dark eyes lighted upon Wulfric, totally ignoring Arietta. Arietta lifted a brow, turning her head to glance at Wulfric over her shoulder.

Wulfric stared down at her in discomfort, shrugging his broad shoulders. He shifted his attention to the other girl. "How is Wendella?"

"There has been no change."

For the first time, the girl noticed Arietta standing beside Wulfric. The smile dropped from her face. "Greetings, Arietta," she said uneasily, peering at Wulfric over Arietta's head.

"Greetings, Estrith."

Estrith threw her brown curls over her shoulder, placing one slender hand on a trim hip. The two women studied each other briefly before Wulfric hastily interrupted. "I thank you, Estrith, for staying with Wendella. I would like to pay you for your service."

She batted her eyelashes at him coyly, and he saw Arietta roll her eyes expressively.

"That is not necessary, Wulfric," the other girl told him shyly. "I was pleased to help you."

Estrith stood smiling at Wulfric, and he shifted his feet nervously, wondering how to get the other girl to leave. Arietta was the one who finally solved his dilemma. She turned to the other girl with a false smile. "Was there something else that you needed to tell us, Estrith?"

Estrith pulled her gaze away from Wulfric, frowning slightly at Arietta. "No, there was nothing else. I had better be leaving now." She turned back to Wulfric, her smile broadening across her pretty face. "If you need me again, Wulfric, just call."

Wulfric said nothing as she passed him.

Arietta watched his expression closely, but his face gave nothing away. Estrith was a very lovely girl, and it suddenly occurred to her that she was inordinately jealous.

When Wulfric set his attention upon her, she hastily averted her face, hoping that he would not notice her feelings reflected there. She wanted to know how well Wulfric knew the girl, but she was afraid to ask.

As though he could discern her thoughts, Wulfric told her, "Estrith's father is a fine combmaker."

Arietta kept her back to him. "He is at that."

"I have done much business with him, as have the others. In our country, combmakers are held in high regard."

With their long hair and beards, Arietta could well understand why. The strained silence which followed was suddenly broken by a moan from the other room. Both Arietta and Wulfric hurried to the room where Wendella lay. Wulfric took Arietta's arm before she could enter the room. His face was bleak.

"You had better let me go first."

She nodded, her eyes fixed on the figure in the bed. In the semidarkened room, all she could see was a body swathed in bandages.

Wulfric entered, carefully sitting down on the bed next to Wendella. She turned her face his way, but her eyes were covered by bandages. She lifted bandaged hands to feel her face.

"What happened?"

Her voice sounded muffled through the strips of cloth binding her face. She grew suddenly agitated. "Wulfric, what happened!"

When she tried to sit up, Wulfric held her firmly down. Her panic began to communicate itself to him, and he attempted to soothe her fears. "Wendella, there was a fire. Do you remember?"

She lay motionless several seconds before jerking into an upright position. Instantly, she placed a bandaged hand to her head and dropped back to the pallet.

"Godfred! Where is Godfred?" she cried.

Wulfric heard the rising hysteria in her voice. He gently lifted her into his arms until she sat across his lap.

"Wendella," he began, still hesitating to tell her the truth.

"Tell me!" she screamed, and if not for her condition, Wulfric knew that she would be pounding his chest in frustration.

"Wendella, Godfred is dead."

Her body stiffened in his arms. She shook her head from side to side in denial. "No! I do not believe you!"

Wulfric stroked a finger across her trembling lips. "Yes, you do," he whispered. "You know that I would never lie to you."

Her body suddenly crumpled against him. Heartrending sobs tore from her throat, tearing at Wulfric's composure. His glinting eyes met Arietta's sympathetic ones.

"Oh, Godfred, Godfred," Wendella moaned, pushing out of Wulfric's arms. She rolled over on the mat, turning her back to him. Her sobs turned to sniffles, and she lashed out in anger. "Go away," she cried harshly.

"I cannot do that," Wulfric answered her softly. "You need someone to care for you."

"I do not need anyone! I do not need you, especially. Just go away!"

"Wendella. . ."

She sat up suddenly, once again trying to feel her face with her bandaged hands.

"What has happened to me?" She tried to pull the cloth strips from her face, but Wulfric stopped her.

"Let me go!" she screamed again, trying to jerk her wrists from his restraining hands. "I want to see."

Wulfric felt a hand on his shoulder and looked up to find Arietta just behind him. Her eyes met his, and he understood her message. He got to his feet and allowed her to take his place.

"Wendella."

Wendella stilled at the new voice.

"Who is that?"

"Arietta."

"What are you doing here? Go away!"

Arietta's lips twitched. "This is my home. They brought you here after the fire."

She digested this news in silence, then abruptly threw back the covers. "Well, take me back."

Arietta placed a restraining hand on her arm. "We cannot, Wendella. There is nowhere to take you back to. Your hut is no more."

Wendella sat still for a few seconds, assimilating this message. She slowly dropped back against the mat, groaning with a mixture of frustration, rage, and pain. Tears fell from beneath the bandages surrounding her eyes.

Arietta brushed a hand lightly over Wendella's. "It is all right, Wendella. I want you to stay with me."

Wendella jerked her hand away, turning away from them once again. She continued to sob quietly. "I do not want to stay with you. I do not want anything from you."

Wulfric and Arietta exchanged worried glances.

"Wendella," Wulfric said softly. "It is kind of Arietta to offer you her hospitality."

There was silence for several long moments. Finally, Wendella rolled toward them. When she spoke, her voice was quietly controlled. "Wulfric, please bring me a knife."

Arietta glanced at Wulfric, her brow furrowed in perplexity. His jaw was tight, a tick forming in his cheek. His eyes grew dark with suppressed feelings. "I will not."

It was then that Arietta realized what Wendella was asking. She turned to the other girl in horror. "Oh, Wendella. You do not want to do something foolish."

"It would not be foolish," she lashed out. "I am deformed, am I not?"

Both Arietta and Wulfric were reluctant to admit to it.

"It may not be as bad as it seems when the wounds heal," Arietta told her hesitantly.

"You do not really believe that. I can hear it in your voice."

"And if you are, so what?" Wulfric decried harshly. "As I have tried to tell you for years, there is more to life than good looks."

"What kind of life?" she yelled back. "What kind of life can I have? No man will ever want me. I will have to live alone for the rest of my life!" Her voice dropped, and the tears threatened again. "I do not even have Godfred."

Arietta quickly left the room. She returned moments later mixing a potion of herbs in a cup of berry juice. She knelt beside Wendella.

"I fixed you a drink, Wendella," she told her, trying to lift the girl's head to help her drink it.

Wendella weakly pushed the cup away, turning her head to the side. "I do not want it."

"It will help to relieve the pain," Arietta soothed.

"I said I do not want it!"

Wulfric took the cup from Arietta, pushing her to the side. The look on his face would have terrified Arietta had she been on the receiving end of it.

"Drink it!" he commanded, placing one large hand behind Wendella's head and holding the cup to her lips.

For a minute, Arietta thought Wendella would refuse, but then she placed one hand on Wulfric's wrist and slowly drank the brew. She wrinkled her nose in distaste. "What was that?"

"Something to help you sleep," Arietta told her, pulling the blanket over her chest. "Try to rest, Wendella. You will feel better in the morning."

Arietta wondered if she had just uttered a lie, but because her voice had been firmly compelling, Wendella settled back against the mat. Before long, they heard her even breathing.

When they returned to the other room, Arietta looked about her in indecision. There were things she needed to do, but she also needed to get back to Gwyn.

"Do not worry. I will take care of things here," Wulfric told her.

She nodded, without really looking at him. Her thoughts were a million miles away. Wulfric placed a hand on her shoulder, and she turned startled eyes to him. "What are you thinking?"

She looked at him sadly. "Will she really try to kill herself?"

Wulfric took a deep breath, turning away from her searching look. He went to the fire pit, adding more fuel and kneeling to stir the ashes.

"I do not know," he said quietly.

Arietta went and sat down across from where he was kneeling. "We have to stop her. Life is too precious."

"She is right, Arietta. What kind of life will she have

even if she does survive?"

She flashed him an appalled look, and he lowered his head. "She is alive and whole. Who is to say what God has in mind for her?"

Wulfric fixed her with a murderous eye. "What purpose did your God have for allowing this to happen? Godfred chose to follow Him, and He allowed him to be slain. Is Wendella's future the price she has to pay for rejecting Him? What kind of God do you follow?"

Arietta's anger grew to match his. "And what about your Thor? What does he ask of you but to die like a Norseman! Your people are slain every day. They murder every day. What kind of god do *you* follow?"

Wulfric stared at her helplessly. "I thought your God was different."

His hollow voice sent chills through Arietta. She leaned forward. "He *is* different. Godfred already knows that. He is in a much better place."

"And Wendella?" he asked bitterly.

"Wendella is like everyone else. We all make our choices. God did not make Wendella rush into that fire to save her brother. Her love did. It was her choice."

Wulfric sighed, leaning back against a bench. He lifted his face to the ceiling, closing his eyes and clenching his hand into a fist.

"But what happens now?"

Arietta shook her head, shrugging her shoulders. "I do not know. I will pray for Wendella, and perhaps the Lord will answer me favorably."

A knock on the door interrupted them. Arietta opened it to find Edwynn leaning against the frame, his face white with exertion. His right arm was still firmly bandaged to his side, and a spot of bright red was forming near the shoulder. Arietta's eyes widened in shock.

"Edwynn, what are you doing here? You should not be out of bed!"

Wulfric pulled Arietta aside in time to catch Edwynn as he fell toward the floor. He lifted the other man effortlessly in his arms, setting him on the recently vacated bench.

Edwynn swayed back and forth slightly until his reeling head became steady once again. Arietta clucked around him like a mother hen, but Edwynn brushed aside her concern.

"I heard that Wendella was here and that she was hurt. I came to see how she is."

Arietta's glance caromed off Wulfric's. "She is asleep. What did you hear?"

Edwynn let his look slide from one to the other. "That there was a fire and that Wendella was burned. How bad is it?"

Arietta fixed her eyes on her fingers twining together in her lap. "It is pretty bad, Edwynn," Arietta answered him softly. "She will be scarred for life."

Edwynn stood up, his eyes glinting. "I want to see her."

Wulfric folded his arms across his chest, his stance belligerent and protective. "I do not think that is a wise idea."

Edwynn faced him unflinchingly. "I intend to see her, whether you allow it or not."

Arietta saw Wulfric's brow rise insolently, a sneer marking his mouth. His challenging gaze met Edwynn's, but the other man did not flinch from that scalding look. Arietta took matters into her own hands. "I think he should, Wulfric."

Wulfric turned to her in surprise, his arms unfolding and dropping to his side. He searched her eyes, then stood aside to allow Edwynn to pass.

Arietta took Edwynn into the room, watching as the smith knelt beside the sleeping mat. Edwynn's eyes grew tender as he stared down at the swathed figure.

"She will not take kindly to being an invalid," he said softly.

Arietta watched his expression closely. "She asked Wulfric for a knife."

He jerked his look back to her. "For what purpose?"

"Wulfric thinks she wants to end her life."

Edwynn's brown eyes turned even darker. He looked back

at Wendella, then rose to his feet. Arietta couldn't miss the look of pain that flashed through his eyes.

"Are you staying with her?"

Arietta shook her head, wrapping her arms around her waist. "No, Wulfric is."

His eyes flashed to hers. "What?"

Realizing that Edwynn had no idea of recent occurrences other than the fire, she explained what had transpired with Gwyn and the others. His look returned to Wendella, and he stood staring at her for some time.

"I am staying with Sidroc and Gwyn until she is able to be on her feet again."

Arietta couldn't interpret Edwynn's look. "And Wulfric is staying here with Wendella?"

She nodded, and Edwynn drew in a deep breath. "Then I will stay as well."

Arietta started to argue, but then thought better of it. When Edwynn looked at Wendella, his face softened, and Arietta realized that despite the accident and the fact that he had committed himself to her, he was still in love with the other girl.

Surprisingly, Wulfric had no objections to Edwynn's staying. If anything, Wendella's accident seemed to have helped the two to call a truce.

When Arietta finally decided to leave, Wulfric rose to his feet. "I will see you to Gwyn's."

Arietta placed her hands on her hips in exasperation. "There is no need. The trader is long gone, and there is no one else who would wish me harm."

Edwynn looked at her seriously. "I would listen to Wulfric, if I were you."

Arietta glowered at him, telling him with her eyes to mind his own business. Edwynn glanced at Wulfric.

"The fire was no accident. One of the villagers told me that Aelwyn set it."

thirteen

The sadness in Gwyn's eyes lingered long after the loss of her child, but life went on. It was the way of the world.

The cold month of November gave way to the slightly colder month of December. The villagers began to look forward to Christmas and its much awaited revelry. They gathered together their supplies of dried fruits and vegetables, hunted for game, and decorated their cottages with the scents of the forest pines.

Arietta and Gwyn traipsed through the forest, collecting pine boughs with which to decorate their houses. It was the first time in ten years that Arietta would have her sister with her, and even though her father would be missing, she was looking forward to celebrating.

Gwyn lifted a green branch to the sun, checking for deformities. Pleased with the almost perfect symmetry, she added the branch to her growing stack. She glanced at Arietta, hacking away at a minute branch of a small pine tree. "I have been meaning to ask," she said, "how is Wendella?"

Arietta paused in her work. She straightened, turning a dubious face to her sister. "I do not know. At times she seems fine, at others she falls into fits of melancholy." She shrugged. "I wish I knew how to help her. Actually, Edwynn seems to have reached her when Wulfric and I have not been able to, but even he has not been able to reach her totally."

Gwyn lifted her pile of branches, indicating that she was ready to leave. Arietta followed suit, walking morosely by Gwyn's side.

Gwyn smiled sympathetically. "You have done a lot for her already, Arietta. Given the way she has treated you, you would have every right to turn her out. Even now, she treats you like a servant who is beneath her."

Arietta's forehead wrinkled. What Gwyn said was true. It had been a test of her faith over the last several weeks to offer Wendella the hospitality of her home when the girl had made it plain at every opportunity what she thought of Arietta. Still, there had been little incidents to encourage her that Wendella might some day accept not only Arietta but her God as well.

"Does she listen to Edwynn?" Gwyn wanted to know.

"She refuses to allow him to see her, but she perversely looks forward to his coming to the house." Arietta shifted the pine boughs in her arms. "Her wounds have healed, but the scars are still there. In time they will fade some, but she will never be the beauty she was. I think that is what bothers her the most. She is afraid if Edwynn sees her, he will be repelled and never return."

"And do you think so?"

Arietta stared off into space, thinking. "I do not believe so. I believe he truly loves her."

The timber of Gwyn's voice changed. "And where does that leave you?"

Arietta laughed without mirth. "Exactly where I was before."

Gwyn was silent for a long time. When she spoke again, it was with some indecision. "Not quite the same. You have Wulfric."

Sighing, Arietta cut her eyes toward her sister. "I do not *have* Wulfric."

"In his eyes you do." Gwyn spoke with certainty.

Arietta sighed again. "I cannot be concerned for myself right now. I need to find a way to reach Wendella with the truth. She needs Jesus' healing power in her life. If only she would accept Him, and I mean *truly* accept Him, into her life."

Gwyn lifted a brow at Arietta. "I heard that she had been baptized."

Arietta frowned. "She would not have been allowed to stay

otherwise, but she does not really believe."

Gwyn stopped, forcing Arietta to stop with her. "Arietta, what do you mean by *truly* believe?"

"Gwyn, in the Scriptures it says that you must believe in your heart, with your *whole* soul, mind, heart, and being. There are so many things in God's Word that could help us all, teach us all, but it is so hard when we can't read the very words of God Himself."

Puzzled, Gwyn frowned. "But the priests will mediate for us, is this not so?"

Arietta hesitated, afraid that she was overstepping her bounds, but the truth was the truth. "The Scriptures say that there is only one mediator between God and man, and that is Christ Jesus."

Gwyn's mouth dropped open. "It truly says this? Then why do the priests say otherwise?"

Shrugging, Arietta continued on her way. "I do not know, and I am afraid to ask any more questions."

The one time she had asked Brother Bertrand, she had been commanded to silence. Ever since, he had not allowed her to copy any more of the Scriptures. Perhaps someday someone would copy the Scriptures into the language of the common people, and they would have copies of their own. She prayed so but wasn't convinced that it would ever happen.

They finished their journey in silence. Arietta left Gwyn at her house and continued on to the village. She was almost there when a figure stepped out from behind a tree. Heart pounding with fright, Arietta stopped short. When the man came out from the shadows, she barely recognized his emaciated form. Her eyes widened, and she dropped her pine branches, hurrying to his side. "Aelwyn!"

The young man stood staring at her, his eyes glazed with fever. He reached out and took her by the arms. She could feel his body shaking through his gripping hands. "Arietta, I am glad to see you well."

His unkempt hair hung to his shoulders, and his face

sported a short, unsightly beard. Arietta lifted a hand, stroking her fingers lightly over his jaw. "You are ill!"

He shook his head slightly. "I will be fine."

"Where have you been? Is it true that you set fire to God-fred's home?"

His face darkened, and at his look, Arietta was suddenly afraid. She tried to move out of his grasp, but his fingers tightened their hold, surprising her with their strength.

"Yea, I killed the Viking. As I intend to kill every one of them."

Arietta's heart dropped at his toneless words, icy fingers of fear running over her entire body. "But Aelwyn, that is *wrong*. You must not do such a thing."

He gritted his teeth, his fingers digging more forcefully into her flesh. "Wrong? I will tell you what is wrong! It is wrong that these heathens come here and take our women and our land. Someone must stop them."

He pulled Arietta closer, his fever-bright eyes roaming her face. His smile sent curls of fear twisting through her stomach. His voice lowered to a whisper. "They have bewitched you, Arietta, but I will save you."

Arietta stood frozen to the spot, her eyes growing wide with terror. Aelwyn was truly mad. Wulfric had been right after all. Aelwyn's grief had twisted his mind and warped his soul. She wasn't certain if it was the fever speaking or whether he had truly lost all reason. She did not think she could deliberate with him in such a condition, but she had to at least try.

"Aelwyn," she coaxed softly, "there is nothing to fear from the Norsemen who have come here. They are our friends."

She knew she had said the wrong thing the minute the words were out of her mouth. His face grew stormy with wrath, his mouth pressed into a tight line. His fingers tightened their hold until Arietta cried out with pain.

"They have bewitched you, but I will take you to the priest and have him exorcize you. Then you will be free, and you can help me show the others. They will listen to you. They have always listened to you."

Taking him by surprise, Arietta pulled away, but Aelwyn's fingers snaked out, clamping around her wrist like a vise. He turned, pulling her with him toward the forest.

"I will not hurt you, Arietta. I only want to help you."

Arietta pulled against his hold, struggling to free herself. She tugged ineffectually at his fingers, trying to pry them loose. "Aelwyn, please! Listen to me!"

He ignored her. They were almost to the forest when a shrill whistle was followed by a strong thud, and an ax seemed to sprout from the tree by Aelwyn's head. Startled, he released his grip, turning to face the intruder. Arietta quickly stepped out of his reach, turning also.

Wulfric stood about twenty feet away, his face a mask of stone. Death glittered from his icy blue eyes. Arietta saw and placed herself protectively in front of Aelwyn.

"Wulfric, he is mad. He is not responsible for what he is doing."

Wulfric's lethal voice froze her insides.

"In my country, we slay mad animals."

Arietta's terrified look shifted to Aelwyn. He stood behind her, his own eyes glittering with the same emotion as Wulfric's. Neither man seemed aware of her presence, both intent upon a course of action that she couldn't allow. Hot air spewed from both men's mouths as their breathing intensified.

Arietta wasn't sure what to do. She tried once more to reason with Wulfric, knowing that his insanity was but a fleeting thing. "Wulfric, please."

He barely glanced her way.

Before Arietta knew what was happening, Aelwyn reached out to snatch her to his side. He pulled Wulfric's ax from the tree in one swift movement, grinning maliciously at the Norseman. "Come, Norseman. Meet your death."

Arietta turned her pleading eyes on her childhood friend. She looked over her shoulder, a mixture of pain and sorrow in her look.

"Please, Aelwyn, do not do this. Let me go. Let me help you."

He glanced down at her, and for the briefest of seconds, his eyes softened. Wulfric moved, and Aelwyn jerked his attention back to the Norseman, his eyes hardening once more. "You have bewitched her, but you will not have her." He looked down at Arietta once again, his look accusing. "I saw the two of you in the forest kissing."

He saw Arietta's face flame with color, and Aelwyn turned a sly smile on Wulfric. "I have heard about your black magic. Call on Thor all you want, but I will release Arietta from your power. If the priest cannot do it, then I will kill her and have the priest pray her soul into heaven."

Wulfric's face blanched. His fingers clenched into fists at his side, and he reached into his leggings and slowly pulled out a long knife.

Seeing his intent, Arietta cried out. "Do not kill him, Wulfric, I beg you."

Wulfric's darkened gaze fastened on her, a tick forming in his cheek. "He killed Godfred and almost killed Wendella. Now he wants to kill you. I cannot allow him to live. If I do, he will slay every one of us."

"He is mad. Brother Bertrand will help him, only please do not kill him and bring that sin upon yourself."

Aelwyn's arm tightened around her waist, pushing the air from her lungs. "I am not mad!" he denied. "I am the only sane one among you. But that will change."

He started backing toward the forest, and Arietta recognized that he was attempting to use the enclosing trees to protect himself from Wulfric's knife. Wulfric followed.

Before Aelwyn could move very far, Arietta reached out, wrapped her arms around a small pine tree and clung tightly. Thus impeded, Aelwyn growled angrily but had no other option than to let go or stop. He chose to let go. He glared at Arietta angrily. "You are one of them," he hissed. "So be it."

He lifted Wulfric's ax, and Arietta cringed, closing her eyes against the death blow that she knew was certain to come.

Hearing a noise from an unexpected direction, she looked up to see Wulfric drop his knife to the ground, and lunge forward as Aelwyn's arm came down. Both men crashed to the forest floor, the ax falling uselessly to the ground at Arietta's feet.

Wulfric struggled with the other man, but Aelwyn's madness gave him strength he would not normally possess. Twisting and rolling, Wulfric finally had the advantage, sitting astride Aelwyn's splayed form.

Wulfric's fingers closed around the other man's throat, gripping tightly. A sound like rushing waters thundered through his head, and he could hear nothing else, see nothing else, but the red haze clouding his vision.

It seemed an eternity before other sounds penetrated through to his consciousness. He could hear Arietta's pleading voice as though coming from far away. The words finally clarified, as well as the sound of her weeping. She was pulling against his fingers.

"Please Wulfric, *let go!* You will kill him! God in heaven, make him let go!"

The surrounding forest rushed back in upon his consciousness, and looking down, Wulfric could see Aelwyn's face turning purple beneath his grip, his eyes bulging. With a cry, Wulfric quickly released his grip, getting swiftly to his feet. He stood breathing hard, watching as Arietta bent quickly to minister to the young man.

Arietta's past words came back to Wulfric. If the lad was dead, then he was a murderer, and he would be denied eternity with this God he was just coming to know.

"Is he dead?" he asked tonelessly.

Arietta sighed softly, sitting back on her heels. "No. He is still breathing."

Wulfric closed his eyes. "Thank God."

Arietta looked up at him, smiling with understanding. "Yes, thank God. Help me get him back to the village."

Wulfric gathered his knife and handed Arietta his ax, then stooped to pick Aelwyn up into his arms. The unconscious boy's head lolled to the side. Wulfric followed Arietta, his heart heavy within him. Would he ever be able to overcome these fierce feelings that caused him to turn into a vicious killer? He wanted this peace of heaven that Arietta spoke so much about, but was it possible for someone like him?

"We should take him to Gwyn's. It would not be wise for Wendella to see him just now," Arietta said over her shoulder.

Gwyn and Sidroc were surprised when Arietta opened the door and Wulfric followed her inside, carrying Aelwyn in his arms.

Startled, Gwyn studied the youth. "Aelwyn! What happened to him?"

"I will explain later," Arietta told her. She pointed at a sleeping bench. "Put him there."

Sidroc stepped forward, his blue eyes burning angrily. "No! Get him out of my house!"

Shocked, Arietta turned to him. His tense body was unyielding. "He needs help, Sidroc."

"I do not care. I want him out of my house."

For the first time, Arietta could easily recognize the likeness between the brothers. She glanced at Wulfric for support and was surprised to get it.

"We must revive him first," Wulfric told his brother. "Then we will see if the ealdorman will call a folkmoot to discuss what is to be done with him."

Sidroc glared angrily at the unconscious youth. Gwyn placed a gentle hand upon his arm. "He is Arietta's friend, and mine as well."

Wulfric's nostrils flared, his eyes burning angrily. "He tried to kill Arietta."

Stunned, Gwyn looked at her sister for confirmation. Arietta held out her hands, her face pinched with worry. "He is ill, Gwyn."

Looks passed between the others. Wulfric sat down across from Aelwyn's inert form.

"I am not leaving his side. Go and talk with the ealdorman,

Sidroc. I will take care of things here."

Looking reluctant, Sidroc nevertheless complied. While Wulfric watched Aelwyn, Gwyn went about her duties. She sent the children to the other end of the house to play out of harm's way.

Arietta tended Aelwyn. Purple bruises were forming on his throat, and she stroked her fingers lightly over the spot. She glanced at Wulfric uncertainly. He looked back at her steadily, his face a blank mask.

Taking a rag, she dunked it into the bowl of water that Gwyn provided. She wiped Aelwyn's forehead, then rung the cloth out and placed it around his throat.

She felt Wulfric's intense scrutiny keenly, almost like a physical touch. When he spoke, his voice was ragged. "I have done nothing but cause you pain."

She snapped her head up in surprise. "That is not so."

He snorted, his mouth twisting wryly. "Edwynn, the trader, Aelwyn." His dark eyes met hers.

Arietta smiled slightly. "You saved me from the trader. If not for you, I would be a slave far away by now. I doubt they had trading on their mind when they landed here in the first place. It was only because of you and your people that they were afraid to do otherwise."

She moved to sit next to him, watching his expression carefully.

"As for Edwynn, who is to know what God's will was in the matter? And Aelwyn has hated Norsemen for many a year. That was not your fault."

He reached across and took her hand, turning her palm up and pulling it to his lips. He placed a kiss in her palm and then curled her fingers around it. "I love you, Arietta. I never thought it would happen to me, but it has."

Her heart increased its tempo tenfold at his sudden declaration. Though Arietta's eyes shone with her answering love, she couldn't speak it. She was committed to Edwynn, and Wulfric was still a heathen.

Aelwyn stirred, and Arietta knelt by his side. He slowly opened his fever-bright eyes, turning them her way. "Arietta?" His voice was hoarse from Wulfric's inflicted wound.

She stroked his forehead softly. "Yes, Aelwyn. It is I."

He turned until his look focused on Wulfric. Sudden comprehension filled his features, and he tried to rise. He fell back helplessly.

"Shh, Aelwyn. Do not try to move."

He lifted a hand weakly, letting his fingers glide across her chin. His look was full of contrition. "I beg pardon, Arietta. I never meant to hurt you. I do not know what came over me."

She took his hand, clutching it within her own. Leaning forward, she tried to smile. "I know, Aelwyn. I forgive you."

He turned his head away, staring up at the ceiling. A knot rose and fell in his throat as he tried to swallow. "But will God?"

Her voice was firm with conviction. "Yes, Aelwyn. He will forgive you anything if you but ask. But you must repent and turn from your ways."

Wulfric was caught by her words. Was it true that all one had to do was ask forgiveness, and it would be granted?

Aelwyn's look went past her shoulder to where Wulfric watched them carefully. He glanced back at Arietta, resignation in his eyes.

"I do not want to go to hell, Arietta," he rasped. "Pray for me."

She squeezed his hand harder. "I will pray *with* you, but *you* must do the asking."

He nodded slightly, and with a hoarse voice begged the Lord's forgiveness. Looking relieved, Aelwyn settled back against the bench and closed his eyes. Before long, he was fast asleep.

ও

The folkmoot convened the next day. Though Aelwyn was still weak and ill, he stood before them, ready to receive his punishment.

The ealdorman stroked his beardless chin, studying Aelwyn

with a firm eye. "What have you to say for yourself, Aelwyn?"

"By the Lord, I am guilty both of deed and instigation of the crime with which Wendella charges me."

Though Wendella had refused to attend the council, Sidroc and Wulfric stood resolutely at the rear of the gathering, their arms folded across their chests. Arietta stood beside them, her heart twisted with pain for her childhood friend.

Two other villagers stepped forward, both claiming, "By the Lord, the oath is pure and not false that Aelwyn swore."

The council nodded, the ealdorman leaning back in his chair. "Then we pronounce judgement. Aelwyn, you are ordered to pay a recompense to Wendella of one hundred pieces of silver for the death of Godfred. Along with that, you are to give her a portion of your land. And if there is any more killing, you will be banished from these parts forever."

Aelwyn hung his head, nodding his agreement. When his eyes met Arietta's, she could see that the fever had diminished, and he was once more in his right mind. He was pale and weak, but he would live.

She glanced at Wulfric and Sidroc and found them both watching the youth with glittering eyes. Aelwyn stopped before them and bravely lifted his gaze to meet theirs. "I beg pardon."

Something flickered in Wulfric's eyes, but Sidroc remained unyielding. Glancing once more at Arietta, Aelwyn moved by them.

Wulfric took him by the arm to stop him. Aelwyn looked up at him in surprise and some degree of concern.

"I beg pardon also," Wulfric gritted, and after a brief time, Aelwyn acknowledged him with a hasty nod before departing.

Both Wulfric and Sidroc understood the judgment. Even in their own land, it was not common for a death to be recompensed with a death. Instead, monetary restitution was usually required.

One hundred pieces of silver was a generous amount and would see Wendella well kept for some time.

෧

While Sidroc and Wulfric returned to their own work, Arietta went to her house. She opened the door, to be met by an agitated Wendella. "Well, what happened?"

Arietta took her time answering. Wendella was prone to fly into fits of rage when things did not go her way. Dropping her cloak on the chair, Arietta knelt and began warming her hands by the fire. She looked, really looked, at Wendella for the first time in days. For some time she had avoided it due to Wendella's sensitivity, but now she took the time to really study the girl.

Wendella's hair was short and hung about her head like a cap. After seeing herself in a bucket of water one day, she had run home, grabbed Arietta's shears, and hacked off her remaining hair. Now, the two layers were almost even, curling to her head in a shimmering moon white mass.

Though one side of her face was clearly marked red by scars, it no longer looked as gruesome as it had before. The trouble was, Arietta couldn't convince Wendella of that.

Arietta gazed into the fire. "You have been allotted one hundred pieces of silver and a portion of Aelwyn's land."

Wendella's hands clenched into fists, her blue eyes igniting with fury. "That is all? That is all that is to be done?"

Arietta frowned at her in exasperation. "What more do you want? Aelwyn's death?" Seeing the look in the other girl's eyes, Arietta shook her head sadly. "Aelwyn's death will not bring Godfred back, Wendella. Aelwyn has asked forgiveness of God."

"God will not forgive him," she declared roundly. "He murdered a man."

Arietta got to her feet, her anger rising. "Murder is no greater a sin than adultery. Gwyn told me about your attempts with Sidroc."

Wendella dropped her gaze, her face flushing with guilty color. "Nothing happened between us."

"But not for your lack of trying. Even among your people,

adultery is a far greater sin than murder. But in God's eyes, a sin is a sin. He has forgiven Aelwyn, and He will forgive you also, if you ask."

Wendella met her look defiantly. "Why should I? I did nothing wrong."

"Not with Sidroc," Arietta answered softly, and the other girl once again hung her head. "But there were others, were there not?"

Wendella's voice rose hysterically. "You do not understand! No one has ever loved me the way that Sidroc loves Gwyn, nor the way that Wulfric loves you. They want to make love to me, but they do not truly. . .love me."

Her voice softened on the last two words, and Arietta stared at her in stunned surprise. It had never occurred to her that Wendella, with her flawless beauty, would feel unloved. It was a disturbing revelation.

"I do."

Startled, they turned to find Edwynn standing in the opened doorway. Wendella drew in a sharp breath and quickly turned away. Edwynn met Arietta's eyes briefly before crossing to where Wendella stood cowering away from him. He reached out but let his hand fall to his side.

"Do not hide from me, Beloved," he said huskily.

Wendella's body stiffened. She remained turned away from him, a small sniffle escaping. "Do not look at me. I am ugly."

He reached out and turned her around. She tried to keep her scarred face from him, but he held her chin firmly with his fingers.

"Not to me," he told her steadily, and looking into his eyes, Wendella must have seen something that told her he spoke the truth. She smiled slightly.

Edwynn touched her lips with a gentle finger. "It is the one thing that gave me hope that you could learn to love me too. Before, you were so. . .so untouchable."

She wrapped her slender fingers around his wrist. "I was a fool," she told him softly.

Realizing that neither one remembered she was in the room, Arietta left the cottage and gently closed the door behind her.

She found Wulfric waiting outside for her, a Wulfric she hardly recognized. He had shaved his beard and trimmed his hair in the way of the English. Her mouth dropped open, and he lifted an eyebrow, his mouth tilting wryly.

"It is time we become one people," he told her firmly.

Arietta could only stare. He was even more handsome than she had remembered. His second brow rose to join the other. "Well, say something."

"Does. . .does Sidroc agree?" she asked in a shocked whisper.

He grinned. "Even now, Gwyn is putting a knife to his throat." His face sobered, and he looked over her shoulder. "What about Wendella?"

Arietta smiled slightly. "I think she and Edwynn have finally come to an understanding."

His eyes took fire. "Then you are free?"

She nodded her head slightly, and he reached forward, pulling her into his arms. He held her so close, she could barely breathe. "I have prayed to God that it would be so. I can see how from tragedy He has brought us all to this point where we truly have what we ask for. At first I did not see, but now it is very clear to me."

Arietta stiffened in his arms. She pulled slightly away, seeking the answer to an unasked question in her eyes.

"Brother Bertrand baptized me," he said softly.

Arietta's green eyes shone with excitement. "Oh, Wulfric."

He smiled, pulling her closer. "He has also said that he would marry us today."

She pushed against his chest, her mouth turning up into a pout. "You were very sure of yourself."

He tilted her chin, stroking a finger over her pouting lips. His glittering eyes smiled into hers. "My love, *you* are the one who taught me about faith. I trusted, and I believed."

Arietta felt tears come to her eyes. "Oh, Wulfric. I love you so much."

"As I do you," he declared. He closed his lips over hers, searing her with the depth of his love. "Now, let us find Brother Bertrand," he told her huskily. "I do not wish to wait one more day before making you my own."

As they walked along hand in hand, a raven flew to the trees above them. Wulfric smiled tightly. "I no longer need your symbols of luck," he told the dark bird. "Be gone, messenger of Odin. The Lord is my salvation now."

The bird cocked its head at them, its beady eye following their movement. After several seconds, it let out a raucous squawk and suddenly flew off into the grey sky. As it disappeared into the distance, a bright ray of sun shone from the hovering clouds, surrounding Wulfric's and Arietta's embracing forms in a halo of brilliant light.

A Letter To Our Readers

Dear Reader:

In order that we might better contribute to your reading enjoyment, we would appreciate your taking a few minutes to respond to the following questions. We welcome your comments and read each form and letter we receive. When completed, please return to the following:

Rebecca Germany, Fiction Editor
Heartsong Presents
PO Box 719
Uhrichsville, Ohio 44683

1. Did you enjoy reading *Viking Pride* by Darlene Mindrup?
   ☐ Very much! I would like to see more books
      by this author!
   ☐ Moderately. I would have enjoyed it more if

   _____

   _____

   _____

2. Are you a member of **Heartsong Presents**? Yes ☐ No ☐
   If no, where did you purchase this book? _____

   _____

3. How would you rate, on a scale from 1 (poor) to 5 (superior), the cover design? _____

4. On a scale from 1 (poor) to 10 (superior), please rate the following elements.

   _____ Heroine   _____ Plot

   _____ Hero   _____ Inspirational theme

   _____ Setting   _____ Secondary characters

5. These characters were special because_____

    _____

    _____

6. How has this book inspired your life?_____

    _____

    _____

7. What settings would you like to see covered in future
    Heartsong Presents books?_____

    _____

    _____

8. What are some inspirational themes you would like to see
    treated in future books?_____

    _____

    _____

9. Would you be interested in reading other **Heartsong
    Presents** titles?   Yes ❑   No ❑

10. Please check your age range:
    ❑ Under 18   ❑ 18-24   ❑ 25-34
    ❑ 35-45   ❑ 46-55   ❑ Over 55

Name _____

Occupation _____

Address _____

City _____ State _____ Zip _____

Email _____

NEW MEXICO *Sunrise*

*J*oin the Lucas, Monroe, and Dawson families as they stake their claim to the "Land of Enchantment." Their struggles and triumphs blend into the sandstone mesas and sweeping sage plains of New Mexico, and their tracks are still visible along the deeply rutted Santa Fe Trail and the chiseled railways they traveled. Award-winning author Tracie Peterson brings their stories to life.

NEW MEXICO *Sunset*

*T*he saga of the Lucas, Monroe, and Dawson families, introduced in *New Mexico Sunrise*, echoes across the vast open landscape of a state in its infancy. Now the next generation must take up the pioneer spirit of their parents and lay claim to their place in a changing world.

paperback, 464 pages, 5 ³⁄₁₆" x 8"

❤ ❤ ❤ ❤ ❤ ❤ ❤ ❤ ❤ ❤ ❤ ❤ ❤ ❤ ❤ ❤

Please send me _____ copies of *New Mexico Sunrise* and _____ copies of *New Mexico Sunset*. I am enclosing $5.97 for each. (Please add $2.00 to cover postage and handling per order. OH add 6% tax.)

Send check or money order, no cash or C.O.D.s please.

Name_____

Address _____

City, State, Zip _____

To place a credit card order, call 1-800-847-8270.
Send to: Heartsong Presents Reader Service, PO Box 721, Uhrichsville, OH 44683

❤ ❤ ❤ ❤ ❤ ❤ ❤ ❤ ❤ ❤ ❤ ❤ ❤ ❤ ❤ ❤

Hearts♥ng Presents
Love Stories Are Rated G!

That's for godly, gratifying, and of course, great! If you love a thrilling love story but don't appreciate the sordidness of some popular paperback romances, **Heartsong Presents** is for you. In fact, **Heartsong Presents** is the *only inspirational romance book club* featuring love stories where Christian faith is the primary ingredient in a marriage relationship.

Sign up today to receive your first set of four never-before-published Christian romances. Send no money now; you will receive a bill with the first shipment. You may cancel at any time without obligation, and if you aren't completely satisfied with any selection, you may return the books for an immediate refund!

Imagine. . .four new romances every four weeks—two historical, two contemporary—with men and women like you who long to meet the one God has chosen as the love of their lives. . .all for the low price of $9.97 postpaid.

To join, simply complete the coupon below and mail to the address provided. **Heartsong Presents** romances are rated G for another reason: They'll arrive *Godspeed!*